Izzy is a 21-year-old girl from Moate, Ireland. Her whole life, Izzy has enjoyed writing. She now lives in Dublin and studies Mental Health Nursing in Trinity. Her main loves in life are travelling and making strangers friends. Her hobbies include pole dancing, collecting pineapple-shaped stuff and eating Reese's peanut butter cups.

For girls, all of you, everywhere. Always stay somewhere between delusion and ambition.

Izzy Hodder

SOMEONE LIKE YOU

AUSTIN MACAULEY PUBLISHERS™

LONDON • CAMBRIDGE • NEW YORK • SHARJAH

A CIP catalogue record for this title is available from the British Library.

ISBN 9781528915182 (Paperback)
ISBN 9781528915199 (Hardback)
ISBN 9781528961141 (ePub e-book)

www.austinmacauley.com

First Published (2019)
Austin Macauley Publishers Ltd
25 Canada Square
Canary Wharf
London
E14 5LQ

I should probably start my acknowledgements with a big thank you to where the whole inspiration for *Someone Like You* came from. I was on YouTube and I came across (somehow!?) a massive amount of video of young girls telling their own stories of becoming pregnant young. It made me realise how underrepresented the topic is. Why didn't we have more books dedicated to these amazing young women? I didn't know why, so I wrote one. So thank you to all of you brave girls who told their stories to the world.

My incredible family also all deserve a thank you.

My Tomato, who opened my manuscript, read for a second, turned to me and said deadpan, 'Engaging first line Izz.' Thank you for the endless support and probably being the only person who ever called me funny.

My little man, I think you're going to write some amazing books one day, but until then thanks for offering to give me the epic stories that enter your head....I'm going to let you write them though. I'm not sure I fully understand.

Of course, my B.B cream, you are a series in yourself. Thanks for never ever failing to make me smile.

To my mom, who let me write a book instead of studying for my Leaving Cert. and always encouraged me to be the most me there is. Because of that, *Someone Like You* exists. My love for you is bigger than anything. Sun, stars and moons.

For my father dearest, I know you're waiting for the day I write a bestseller about rocks. You'll be waiting a while so thank you for supporting my other crazy stuff.

To Kylie, for being a beautiful person inside and out. You are so selfless and so kind.

To Eamon, whose advice I'd pretend to always ignore but really did listen to. Thank you for giving me Alucard, that was my first book to finish and that started it all.

And, of course, for all the rest of my family, my pretend brother. Ben/Eoinie, thanks for never writing back (it made me write more), being a better skier, but a worse dancer (sorry it's true).

I'm blessed to have so many more incredible people and friends I want to thank.

My jellyfish, of course, thank you for simply existing. For reading a page and getting bored but telling me it was amazing anyways. You've got my back before I even tell you what for and for that I can't be thankful enough. Love you, obviously.

DreDra, you listened to every single bizzare book idea of mine on our long walks every day for years. You deserve a medal alone for that. Oh also, the tan, thank you.

To my primary school girls, who are all such characters that I couldn't make up anyone as great as them.

My Bed Buddy/Berlin Wall, for always making me laugh and the best toasties ever.

My Amputee, for letting me dance with your kitchen utensils.

My Edward Cullen, for being a vampire and creating whole new worlds for ourselves to live in. Bites are fun, right?

And my partner in musicals, Jenny, I'll never forget the time we escaped from gay camp.

To an old man who's younger than me (thanks for calling me an egg). Your never-ending support means a lot more than words and we always get them wrong with each other so I won't even try.

To the Bower, all my teachers and the whole class of 2017(just because I love that place so much) and the beautiful people it brought into my life.

My starfish, who always, always believed in me. And made me feel special. You're going so many places.

My pumpkin-spiced latte, you're sweetness and encouragement I'll always love. I have learned so much of it from you.

To Oblin2458, you are always you and that is so, so, so inspiring.

Laina Bear, my partner in riots. You're drive and passion for causes and people is beautiful.

My Megsta, some friendships surprise you with their reliability and love. Ours did this.

And to my lil' gang, just the galz. You girls are support and love in three people. Thank you so much for making me feel at home in a new place.

Now I could go on, and on, but I'll just say this: if you are in my life or ever were in my life, I'm thankful. Also thanks to chance and life for simply me being here and alive.

Prologue

It was a cold February day when I found out I was pregnant. I was seventeen years old. In that moment, my life was changed forever. I'm not the girl you'd expect to get pregnant. I led a sheltered life, a happy life. I wasn't naïve, I knew what I was doing and I knew the risk, I just never thought I'd be in the 3%. Like all of us do every single day, I simply thought, things like that don't happen, to people like me.

Chapter 1
February

It's crazy that the first thing you think about after peeing onto that stick is your parents. It's not yourself or your own future or all the plans and dreams you had. It's your mum's reaction and your dad's face when the realisation hits him. I couldn't do that to them, was my first thought, yet I had was my second. I knew I wouldn't be able to keep it from them for long. The guilt was already growing enormous inside of me. I stood up in the public toilet cubicle. I was in a Starbucks. How bad does that sound. I was in a Starbucks when I found out I was pregnant. Tell that story to your grandkids. I threw the test box and stick into the bin, looked in the dirty mirror, rubbed my tired eyes and walked back out.

"Amy! Hey what took you so long; the guys are waiting at the park for us," cried Lily. I was in a daze. I honestly don't know how I was functioning. I don't think I fully understood what was happening, or about to happen.

"Oh Lily," I froze at the table where her and my other best friend Tara sat sipping Caramel Frappuccinos.

They both stared up at me. "You look kind of pale Amy," said Tara, ever the blunt one bless her.

"I think I'm coming down with the flu," I lied. "I feel awful I might just head home."

"But, Amy wait; this was going to be our last girls night out! You know we won't be out half as much soon, with exams and everything? Are you sure?" Lily argued.

"Thanks Lily, but I'm sure. I need to rest, I'm sorry! I'll see you guys tomorrow, have fun! Love you."

I walked out the door into the cold air of London's February breeze. Mum would be home from work and Dad would be on his way. I had to tell them, they deserved that at least.

The Story of Mum and Dad

My parents were in college when they meet. Dad was doing medicine and Mum was studying to become a nurse. Dad says mum fell for his leather jacket and messy hair, Mum says she's always wanted a doctor for a boyfriend but not a husband but hey that's what happens right. When they started dating in third year of college, everyone called it puppy love. Black and white pictures showed them all over each other at concerts, lectures, college balls, road-trips, everything. They were as thick as thieves, my nanny Rose would say, referring to the many times my dad would somehow be there for breakfast but never there the night beforehand, claiming he had just popped over after his morning run. Neither of them had a relationship before each other. Mum, however, graduated three years before Dad was due to finish. There were loads of jobs for her in Australia and she wanted to travel. I've found her diaries from the time and I almost cry when I read them.

"I can't believe I broke up with Jacob today. It's stupid and soppy but I feel like I'm leaving behind a piece of me. I know Dad doesn't approve of his attitude, or the way he is at times but I love him. I really do, even if I'm leaving him. I'll leave him behind, but he'll never leave me."

Then a couple of weeks later the entries talk of parties and Australian boys; barbecues on the beach and everyone falling asleep around the campfire after work. Mum didn't forget to live, she moved on I think. She even got involved in a short fling with a girl whose eyes she swore held the universe inside them. Meanwhile, Dad was still studying, his friends that he still has from college all say he mopped around, drank too much and failed a couple of exams for a few months before shaking it off and getting into a serious relationship with a girl called Lisa four years younger than him. She was studying tourism and I think he was attracted to her youth and sparkle, something he failed to find in people his age other than my mum. So it had appeared that he had moved on too.

But then exactly one year after Mum moved away; Dad's name popped back up in her diary.

"I decided last night, after too many tequilas, that I needed to move. I'm falling too much here, but not into anything good. Eliza was fun but I don't actually love girls. Josh was great but

13

I mean, he's never going to love something more than his board and that's okay. I think I'm going to move to Melbourne. They say it's colder there and I wouldn't mind buying a few jumpers. A photo I thought I'd lost fell out of an old book I had today. It was of me and Jacob. A part of me still aches when I hear someone say that name, or I think I hear his voice from time to time. It's funny because I thought or think I've moved on but I'll never forget our love. I guess some loves just fade away as time passes, and others, well I guess other loves fade into us as time passes."

Two weeks later Mum moved to Melbourne. She found a job, an apartment and a cat, named Blue because she found it behind her blue bin out the front.

A month later Dad's college offered three students the opportunity to study abroad for a year in a partnering university. Dad won the scholarship and by chance was sent to the University Hospital in Melbourne. He moved there three weeks later.

Two days after Dad arrived in Melbourne, he was rushing on his way to one of his first lectures. He had bought new shoes that kept untying so he was looking down at them.

At the same time, Mum was tying a scarf around her neck with a coffee in her other hand, late for an appointment with the dentist. She wanted braces and had been saving for months.

Neither of them saw each other until Dad leaned down to tie his shoelaces and Mum's scarf flew away from her in the wind and landed at his feet. They looked at each other and that was that.

How do I do it, was all I could think walking home. *What if Mike's home already?* I pulled my key out of my back pocket to open my front door. We lived in one of those typical London houses, five storeys high and narrow with a tiny back garden. Mum had it showered in Dahlias and Daffodils and she even owned another two plots down at the local gardens. Our house always smelled good, and today as I walked in, the fresh scent of poppies hit me straight away. I shrugged off my jacket

"Hello," I called out, no response. I bounded up the stairs only to hear the shower running in my mum's bathroom.

"Yo, Amy."

I spun around, I hadn't seen Mike behind me, he was talking in all this weird slang these days but for a fifteen-year-old-boy, he wasn't too bad.

"Mike, hey," I said taking the next flight of stairs to where my bedroom was.

"Wait, Amy I want to show you my new pictures," he raced up the stairs after me, his laptop underneath his arm.

I sighed, but only mockingly. Really I loved looking at Mike's latest pictures, it was like watching little clues into his life, where he'd been, how he'd captured it.

"Sit down and show me, what old building did we break into this weekend?" I joked, referring to how Mike and his friends were always finding old dilapidated houses and schools to crawl into and wander around, taking actually really good pictures of what they discovered.

"It's crazy Amy you'll never believe what we found down near the wharf! It was like this great old B&B maybe? There were tons of rooms, like eleven stories but it looked just like a normal house! Super creepy and on the inside there was all bedrooms, but some messed up shit definitely happened there."

I interrupted, because when Mike gets excited he can just talk and talk.

"What kind of messed up stuff?" I asked, "And who did you go there with? Doesn't Rob get scared when it gets at all spooky and isn't Liam away with his dad this month?"

I know, who was I to be protective and all in the right when here I was after getting pregnant, but still, he was my little brother.

"Chill Amy, I was there with someone else, anyways it was cool okay."

I nodded.

"Sorry Mike, I didn't mean to snap at you like that, it's, it's been a hectic day."

Mike rolled his eyes and stood up, "what had a fight with your boyfriend or something stupid like that, honestly Amy open your eyes, the worlds a bit bigger," and with that he walked out of my room.

"Arghh," I groaned out loud and flopped back on my bed.

"Amy, is that you hunny?" Mum yelled out, the shower off.

"Yep, I'm home," I yelled back.

She knocked gently on my door before opening it.

"Hey you, tough day at school?" I sat up; my mum was so pretty, even standing there in her towel with her wet hair drying on her shoulders. Her eyelashes were longer when they were wet and her red lips stood out even more against her sallow skin. My heart sank.

"Something like that."

"Aw, well don't worry. I've got your favourite in the oven! If Luke's coming over later that's fine," and with that name's ink left dripping in my mind, she shut the door.

Luke, Luke, oh god Luke, every single inch of me wanted him to be beside me in that moment.

When We Met

"I think you dropped this," said the boy with the glasses and the blonde, floppy hair. He sat behind me in geography. We'd never spoke before. But then again it was only the third week of school. I turned around to see him picking up my bumblebee eraser. I blushed violently. He was cute. I hadn't noticed that before.

"Thanks," I said trying to hide my embarrassment. Of course my first encounter with a boy in my new school would have to involve my beloved bee eraser from 6th grade. I turned back around with a smile. A few moments later there was a tap on my shoulder. Then a folded sheet of paper landed on my desk. I nervously picked it up and unfolded it quietly while the teacher talked about the formation of a volcano.

'Random fact – Did you know bee's communicate by dancing, not too sure how I'd fair if I had to be a bee... ☺'

I smiled and scribbled down something on the back of the folded note and subtly put my hand behind my back. He plucked it out.

This went on for weeks. We rarely spoke or even saw each other much outside of this class. It was the only one we had together that year. One day though I stayed back late in class to talk to the teacher about my last essay. It was last period and when I walked out of the class the boy with the floppy hair was there, I knew now his name was Luke.

"You busy?" He asked stepping into stride beside me as we walked down the hallway.

"Not particularly," I said shyly. I had between 0 and 1 experience with boys to date.

"Great," he shoved his hands into his pockets. "I've somewhere I want to show you, but we better move quick. I'm not sure what time it closes."

I don't know if I knew from the start that there was going to be something different about Luke and me. That over the next two years we were going to defy the odds of arguing over cheating with each other's friends, getting drunk and fighting outside nightclubs, breaking up over text only to get back together a week later. But on that first day, when he lead me on a mystery tour around London, eventually arriving at a miniature indoor bee sanctuary hidden in the centre of Mayfair, on that day I knew I felt something. I knew from books and movies that young loves were supposedly epic, but I had never experienced anything of the sort in my fifteen years on this earth. Yet I knew we were more than the rest. We were going to be different, I just didn't know how yet. That night we bought doughnuts in Soho and got a tube back to my part of the city. He walked me to my house.

"Well I'll see you," I said awkwardly.

"I'll see you too Amy," he replied looking straight at me. He looked nervous.

I nodded feebly and all of a sudden he grabbed my hand and kissed me. I'd kissed a few other boys before. I wasn't that inexperienced. But kissing Luke, even that first time, was kissing the future and the past and the present all at the same time and all of it delving together. My tummy turned and my heart sped up and I knew, I just knew, I was screwed.

Chapter 2

Mum had cooked my favourite. Vegetarian lasagne, but I could hardly manage three mouthfuls. Dad was home from work, him and Mike sitting opposite Mum and I talking about the rugby. Mum nudged my shoulder, "Are you alright? You've barely touched your dinner."

I nodded and scooped a spoonful in my mouth smiling.

The boys chatter stopped. "So Amy," said Dad, "we got your results from your mock exams this morning."

I looked up, shit, I had completely forgotten about them.

"Don't look so worried," Dad laughed, "you did incredibly, especially for someone who went on and on about how unprepared she was!"

"You got all A's and B's Amy! We're so proud," said Mum.

"Even in geography," nodded Dad. "A B."

Mike made a vomiting motion with his fingers and I laughed at him despite myself. Our parents were extremely loving and proud and sometime we couldn't help but laugh.

"Seriously though did I?" I asked.

"Yeah! Trust me sweetie I was as shocked as you," joked Dad, "but we decided that seeing as you've done so well, and we know you will do wonderful in you're A-levels." He looked to Mum who smiled and nodded back at him, "well we've decided, that if you really want to go to Italy with Tara and Lily and the boys this summer then you can."

"What? Are you serious?" I asked.

Italy was a dream trip that I, the girls and Luke and his friends had been planning for months but I was the only one not allowed. Not that any of it mattered now. I don't even know why I was still asking.

"Seriously," said Mum smiling.

I looked around the table, from my smiling mum to my proud dad to my kind, kind little brother. And I broke into tears.

"Oh Jesus Amy, chill out, it's just a freaking holiday," laughed Mike.

"It's not that," I started.

"Amy, what's wrong?"

"I don't know how to say…I said composing myself, Mike looked sick, looking back now I think he knew what I was about to say. I think it was the first thing that popped into his head and he knew. The whole room was silent and I felt like silence had never been so loud before in my life.

"I'm pregnant," I stuttered out. Weirdly enough, once I said those words out loud, a sort of calmness came over me and I was able to look up at my whole family's faces.

Dad was the first to speak, I think my mum was about to faint.

"Amy, what are you talking about?" He paused but I had nothing to say. "Please tell me this is some sort of joke because if you think I raised you to go…" he raised his voice.

"Jacob stop!" said Mum turning to me, "Amy, are you sure?"

"Is she sure? Even the fact that she might be … Amy explain yourself," my dad shouted, I'd never seen him this angry and it scared me. I turned to Mum.

"I took a test, Mum, and it was positive, I mean maybe it is wrong, it could be wrong because…"

"Because what Amy," snapped Dad, his head in his hands. I knew deep down he was just upset, not angry.

"Because," I said quietly, "I'm on the pill and we always use protection, so maybe it got it wrong…"

"Always!" shouted Dad pushing himself up from the table, "You mean to say…" He couldn't finish, I knew what he was thinking though. That his little girl was having sex, she didn't just have it once. He left the room. The back door banged, shaking the house as he left.

Mum, Mike and I sat in silence. Mike still hadn't said a word. I looked down at my plate; my barely touched vegetarian lasagne. I was so privileged, so loved, how could I have let this happen?

Mum let out a sigh breaking the silence.

"I'll take you to the doctor tomorrow, not your dad obviously," she shook her head as if erasing an image and stood up, taking our plates.

"Until then there's no use in getting more upset or angry, and I shouldn't have to even say this but not a word to anyone right Mike?" She looked at my brother sternly. He nodded and with that she walked into the kitchen.

"Amy," Mike said so softly it was almost a whisper.

I looked up at him from behind my ash blonde hair that had fallen over my face.

He reached out his hand across the table, placing it on top of mine. He smiled. I felt a tear roll down my cheek. Mike gripped my hand tighter. We sat in silence, I don't know how long we sat there for but suddenly a cold breeze rushed through the house and a booming voice echoed down from our hallway. Mike's eyes opened. My stomach turned upside down. "Shit," I said accidently out loud.

"Amy who's that..." Mum's voice trailed off as she walked back into the dining room just as Luke let himself in from the hall. Time seemed to freeze as Luke saw me sitting crying at the table with Mike's hand on mine, he quickly took in my mum's red eyes and was about to say something when the back door banged and my dad's voice came clearly towards us

"Okay, we all just need to talk I'm sorry I was just in so much shock I mean you're only seventeen but..." and with that my dad entered the room. I really shouldn't have forgotten to tell Luke not to come over tonight.

"Luke," said my dad sternly, crossing his arms over his chest. I knew it was taking a lot of self-control for him to not start shouting. But as I've said, my parents are good people, strong people, even in the most testing of times.

"Amy..." Luke looked like a bunny in headlights, I'd have laughed at him if the situation weren't so serious.

"What's going on, I'm sorry if I've interrupted a family thing I'll go..." he started to turn around. My stupid mouth wouldn't say the words my brain was articulating.

"No Luke," Mum said suddenly, "Amy..." I knew Mum was torn between punishing me by making me tell Luke here and now and protecting me like she had been doing all my life. I stood up, this was my responsibility now.

"Luke," I stepped towards him despite the look on my father's face getting more and more stern.

"I took a test yesterday and there's no easy way to say this Luke but … I think I'm pregnant."

Silence, yet again. Luke's face was completely blank. His hands swung dead beside him. I could feel the fire begin to bubble inside me. Have some kind or reaction at least god damn it.

"But I don't understand…Amy what the fuck?" Luke said stepping away

"Luke please, I don't know either but…" I went to be closer to him but he shook me off.

"No. What? Are you saying that?" He looked around quickly, "I've got to go," he said and turned away. He had left. Just like that. My heart stung a little, no not a little a lot. Luke and I fought, we weren't perfect people but we never left each other with words unspoken. It was our unwritten pact. I burst into tears. My family didn't move but no one said a word. No one knew what to say, for some things there are no words.

Chapter 3

I woke up the next morning in a cold sweat. In my dream I was sitting in the cinema when a baby started to cry in the back aisle. Then suddenly all the people in the whole cinema were babies. Crying and crying. I shook my head until I woke up, gasping and moaning. My mum was by my side.

"Amy, sweetie shh, it was just a dream you're okay."

I sat up and the whole happenings of the last 48 hours came roaring back into my brain. As you can imagine, I lay back down with a sigh.

"You'd better get up," said Mum, "I've an appointment for us, for you, sorry, at Dr Foster's for 9am." I looked up at my clock, quarter past eight.

"Okay, I'll be down soon, thanks Mum." I smiled and she nodded back; closing the door gently behind her. I reached to my bedside table for my phone. I had a missed call from Luke and one new message.

"Amy I'm so sorry about how I acted. I don't know what came over me. It was just a shock I think. I don't know what to do now so call me when you can. I love you always Amy, I'm sorry I'm a dick sometimes. Okay text me x," I breathed a sigh of relief. So Luke wasn't a complete runner. In truth I hadn't thought he would be but he did scare me for a moment. Through all our time together that was definitely the most shocked I was by his behaviour. I tried to push it out of my mind as I got dressed. He had apologised, everything would be okay. Usually when anything happened with Luke, Tara was my first phone call. But I couldn't do that. Did I want her to know? I didn't know how she would react but I knew she would have the right words. Even if these last few months she hadn't been acting herself. I presumed it was down to stress, her parents were really pushing for her to do medicine and she was studying like crazy.

My Much Braver and Better Best Friend

"You shouldn't listen to them you know," said Tara. *We were eight years old and at the local park near my old school. Our mums were having coffee in a café just across the road. I didn't say anything back.*

"Amy who's your friend, is she as weird as you? I bet she talks to herself too," yelled a snotty red haired girl from the top of the playground castle. Her name was Suzie. She was in my class in school. Tara wasn't in my school but I so ever wished she were. The kids in my school weren't like her. I couldn't talk to them about books or old comic magazines. They thought it was weird. I was so glad Tara's mum and mine were best friends since birth and that they were 'just absolutely determined Tara and Amy would be too!'

"What's her name?" whispered Tara across the seesaw.

"Suzie," I mouthed back.

"Hey Suzie," yelled Tara.

Suzie turned around and slid down the slide but kept her distance. I could see Tara's stout stance and body scared her a little.

"You'd better get yourself to a fire station, before you burn yourself," said Tara confidently. It was a poor feeble dig but we were eight years old and it was enough to leave the popular Suzie speechless, running to the safety of the swings with her hands over her hair. We burst out laughing, hoping off the seesaw.

"My grandma used to tell me mean people are only like that because they're sad so I should feel sorry for Suzie but nobody should do that to my Amy," smiled Tara grabbing my skinny little hands and holding them in her soft comfy ones. *"It'll be okay, when we're older you can move from your side of London to mine and we can go to school together in matching outfits and everyone will be jealous."*

"We'll be invincible," I said, *"and maybe even have superpowers!"*

"Oh yes definitely superpowers, I want to be able to be invisible."

"And I want to be able to fly!"

"Oh everyone will think we are the coolest two girls alive and all the boys will turn into princes when they see us and we will get to pick our favourite!"

I smiled. Tara always made me happy.

"Now race you to the tree and back," she shouted and off we ran; the wind and leaves wiping away any of our worries.

The waiting room was white and sterile as always. I hadn't wanted to come to Dr Foster; she had been my doctor for all matters that didn't go to Dad. I know it was stupid but I didn't want her thinking I was a slut. I was aware I had more to be worrying about than that and things were only going to get harder but still I argued with Mum on the way here but she was insistent that she trusted Dr Foster and we weren't going anywhere else.

"Amy Webb," said the nurse. Mum and I stood up, following her down the hall and into Dr Foster's room.

"Well Amy! How are you? Tough year, how are you holding up?" asked Dr Foster friendlily.

"Oh I'm fine," I said weakly sitting down on the examination bed.

"And you Liz how are things?" she asked my mum and they chattered about work for a minute or so. I could hear the tension in Mum's voice.

"Now Amy what can I help you with?"

"Ehm, well…" I took a breath. "I need a proper pregnancy test I think." It sounded so stupid when I said it. I sounded so childish and unknowing. I guess I was.

"Okay, no problem. We will take your bloods but we will start with a urine test so if you could pop down the hall with this," she handed me a clear cylinder tube with a lid, "and pop back up once you're done." She smiled encouragingly and I went out.

When I returned, Mum's eyes were red and Dr Foster was holding her hand.

"Great Amy, thank you, I'll send that now and we will have your results in the next few minutes' a nurse came in and took the sample. *Great*, I thought, *another person who knows I'm pregnant.* I was thinking completely irrationally, if this was now my life I was going to need to not care.

Dr Foster set up her equipment to take my blood. All the while talking to me about normal things, she was being really kind and I didn't feel as though she was judging me. When we were done, the nurse came back handing Dr Foster a piece of paper.

"Well Amy," her expression was neither a frown nor a smile, "it looks like you are pregnant."

I let out a breath.

"I know this is unplanned and will be a lot to take in, but remember you still have a lot of options open to you."

"I can't have a baby," I said simply, emotionless.

"Oh Amy!" My mum came over and wrapped her arms around me. I started to cry into her shoulder.

"I understand that you'll be having a lot of thoughts but there's no immediate rush. Right now what I would advise is that you go home, rest and have a think. I'd like to see you here again on Monday after school so in two days if that is okay? We will have the blood tests back by then and can discuss our options further, is that okay with you Amy?" She said our options and those two words made me feel very less alone. I nodded, wiping my eyes with the back of my hand.

"Okay Amy," she said softly handing me a tissue. Once Mum and I had both composed ourselves we thanked Dr Foster and left.

In the car I felt a whole lot calmer and I just wanted to watch a funny movie and laugh. Mum was being really kind too.

"I'm not going to tell the girls, no matter what I do," I said to her as we drove after telling her about Luke's text. We were close in that way and I knew I needed her now more than ever.

"That's a hard thing to do Amy, why?"

"We've so many exams and so much of their future lies on this year, I don't want to worry them or distract them with my own problems," I said truthfully.

"That's a really thoughtful decision, I'm proud of you, hey why don't you give Tara a call, I know her mum's been worried about her these days, maybe she could distract you even if she doesn't know she is, or would that be too hard. Am I doing the right thing here Amy I really don't even know… should I even be letting you outside, oh god!" Mum clapped her hands against the steering wheel, her eyes watering.

"It's okay, Mum, I'm sorry there is no right way I don't think but that does sound really nice, will you just drop me off at hers on the way home."

Mum just nodded. I think she was afraid if she spoke she would cry.

I texted Tara to say I was coming over but by the time we pulled up outside her house I had no reply. I told Mum I'd call her if she wasn't there and I bounded around to Tara's back door. We were long past ringing the doorbell with each other. Tara was an only child, as her mum always said I was her second daughter; her favourite one. I let myself in the back door; neither of her parents appeared to be home so I called her name. When I got no response I started up the stairs.

"Tara!" I said pushing open her door and jumping in. no one there. I heard a groaning sound coming from her en suite so I ran to her bathroom door and pushed it open. Tara was kneeling on the floor in front of her toilet, her two fingers pushing down her mouth. She saw me and collapsed.

Chapter 4

"Yes, no I'm her friend not family but please let me see her…I brought her here!"

The lady with the hair sprayed stiff bun pursed her lips and looked down at her desk. The hospital was a buzz of tears, noise and the smell of machine coffee.

"It's against all regulations, I'm sorry we're going to have to just wait."

"Please," I whispered and suddenly there was a strong familiar arm on my back.

"What's going on?" asked Luke as I turned to see him. He kissed me on the forehead. I had called him in tears from Tara's house straight after calling the ambulance.

"Unfortunately, sir we cannot let non-family members in to see a patient before the patient's guardians are present. It's just regulations, I am sorry." I could see her face had softened since she had seen Luke kiss me on the forehead. Acts of young love always softened even the hardest of hearts. I squeezed Luke's hand.

"But her parents aren't even in London, I called them in the ambulance, they went to Kent for the weekend, please they trust me to look after her until they're back. I'm sure they won't be long!"

"Please miss, let my girlfriend see her best friend or can we at least know what's going on?"

The woman sighed, "I'll get the doctor on her ward to come and talk to you okay, please just take a seat over there."

We nodded and Luke led me over to beside the coffee machine, after settling me down he jumped up and came back with two of those awful instants but it was better than nothing right now.

"Amz what happened, I mean how?" He asked sitting down beside me. I nestled into the nook of his arm.

"Luke, I don't even know. All I did was walk in and…" My voice trailed off, I dreaded to think of what Tara was doing leaned over that porcelain toilet. I feared I knew and it made me ill to think about it.

"But she just collapsed?"

I nodded. I wouldn't tell him anything until I knew the facts. Maybe I had read too many books. She was probably just after eating a bad avocado sandwich. I always told her they were bad at this time of year.

"She wouldn't move at first." I started to replay the awfulness of it, "then she started convulsing and seizing on the floor, I was so afraid she would hit her head on the tiles so I pushed a towel underneath her. Oh Luke it was so scary waiting for the ambulance." I started to cry, "I'm so afraid for her."

"Shhh shh, it'll be okay, have you told your parents?" I shook my head.

"Well we should, they could be worried …"

A doctor with a mop of brown hair and kind looking eyes walked over towards us.

"You must be Amy am I right?" he asked kneeling down in front of me. I tucked myself out of Luke and sat upright.

"That's me, is Tara okay can I see her? I know the lady at the desk said I couldn't but…"

The doctor cut me off.

"You brought her in am I right?" he asked looking down at the papers.

"Yes," I replied, annoyed that he had interrupted me though I knew from my dad that doctors were always busy and being a waiting room person was often a godsend for them. I didn't care at this point, I cared about Tara.

"Look Amy I am so sorry but until her parents arrive we can't let you in, anyways Tara is currently asleep. She's on a lot of drugs right now to help her get better."

"But what happened?" I asked, "What's wrong with her?"

"We need to talk to Tara when she wakes up to get a better idea of the situation." He smiled, "hang in there."

And with that he patted my knee and walked away.

"Idiot," muttered Luke.

"Shh," I whispered. "It's true he can't tell us anything it's not his fault. I've watched enough A&E and Grey's Anatomy to know."

Luke smiled. "Oh god, remember that weekend you had chicken pox," he started to laugh.

"Stop that wasn't funny; it hurt so much and I looked awful," I giggled.

"You made me watch ten episodes of Grey's Anatomy with you while you cried into a bowl of ice-cream," he teased.

"Oh god I really did didn't I, how did you ever stick it, you hate hospitals!" I remembered the time well. Luke had just asked me to be his girlfriend after months of us spending every aching moment we could together.

"Oh I don't know, I guess I realised something sitting there watching you cry over people you didn't even know."

"What did you realise?" I asked curiously, sitting up.

Luke sighed and looked ahead, "That you were the kindest person I knew… and that I was falling quite badly in love with you…"

I grinned at him and kissed him on the lips. The lady sitting next to me cleared her throat and I rolled my eyes at Luke who rolled his back.

I settled myself up against him again and fell asleep, ignoring the fact that neither of us mentioned the massive issue of baby, or Tara or anything else horrible and scary to think of. Instead we ignored the surrounding buzz of lives beginning and ending and returned to our safe haven; each other.

I woke with a start half an hour later. Tara's parents had arrived into the waiting room and were demanding answers. Luke straightened himself up, I told him it was probably best for him to go and I would call him later.

Once he left, Tara's mum burst into tears, pulling me close and whispering thank you thank you. The doctor with the kind eyes returned to us.

"Mr and Mrs Lee?" he asked.

Tara's father nodded, his eyes glazed.

"You'll be glad to know Tara has woken up."

We all breathed a sigh of relief.

"We have a specialist psychologist in talking with her now and once they are done we will have a full diagnosis but as of now."

Tara's mum interrupted.

"What kind of specialist, I don't understand, what happened to her?"

"Your daughter suffered a seizure. As a result of malnourishment, we have had nutrient drips going into her for the last hour to build her up again, but unfortunately that is not the solution."

"Malnourishment? But Tara's isn't skinny. She eats like any of us?" said her dad.

"Yes, that's why this is not the permanent solution. We believe Tara is suffering from bulimia nervosa."

Amy's mum sobbed. I stayed silent. The doctor continued.

"It is a very common eating disorder and mostly goes unnoticed unless something like this should happen. People with bulimia nervosa don't usually lose weight or if they do it is only for a short period of time."

I breathed in and out slowly. I was a terrible friend, how could I have not noticed the signs. Then again, a lot of the time we see what we want to see. I held Tara's mum's hand tighter. The doctor told us to sit tight and that he would be back soon.

"Amy darling, thank you so much for everything but I think you should go home," said Tara's dad.

"Oh Amy thank you, we called your mum on our way here and she seemed awful worried. It's probably best if it's just us when Tara is ready anyways, who knows how she will be."

I nodded and hugged them goodbye. I understood what they needed. I would go see Tara tomorrow and there would be no more secrets between us. She needed me now; I had to be strong for the girl who was always strong for me.

Dad collected me outside the hospital five minutes later.

"Hop in," he said gruffly and I did. The whole way home he didn't say a word. He had obviously taken the news that I was definitely pregnant terribly, but why stay mad at me? What good was it doing? When we stopped outside our house he turned off the engine, looked at me as if he were about to say something, then just shook his head and got out.

"Dad," I started to say following him. He put up his hand and walked inside.

The Man Who Would Do Anything for Me

It was the last day of middle school. I was fourteen years old. Skinny, awkward, geeky but most of all, friendless; except for Tara of course but I barely saw her these days. Dad picked me up outside the school while all the other kids sauntered off together to go shopping or get ice creams in West End or whatever it was people who had groups of friends did.

"What's up kiddo?" asked Dad, two minutes in, referring to my silence.

"Everyone thinks I'm a freak," I mumbled so he wouldn't hear me.

"Huh, speak up," said Dad turning down the radio.

"No one likes me, Dad... they all think I'm weird." I looked down at the floor. Dad took a sharp right, heading in the opposite direction to home.

We drove in silence for a while, before pulling up outside a green shop that read in rusty gold lettering 'CUPCAKES FOR SALE'

I looked at Dad.

"Out we get," he said.

I followed him out of the car. We were in a much rougher part of London than I was used to. Dad double-checked he's locked the car. I stayed close to him as we entered the green shop, a bell rung as we went inside.

"Welcome, welcome, what can we do for you today?" asked a tall eastern European woman with a strong accent.

Dad looked down at me.

"We are looking for two, oh no, four of your finest cupcakes please."

"Go on upstairs and they will be with you straight away," said the woman flamboyantly directing us up a creaky old staircase at the back of the shop.

Dad didn't seem phased so I followed him up and we came to a roof garden with an amazing view of the city.

"Dad, this place is so cool! How did you find it?"

"Oh your old man's been around the place," he smiled as we sat down.

"Now listen to me Amy…"

The lady arrived up with our cupcakes; Chocolate fudge, Red Velvet, French Vanilla and Salted Caramel. I looked back up at Dad. He picked up the Red Velvet and started to take off its wrapping.

"There are always going to be people in this world who don't appreciate madness; a bit of insanity. There will always be people who will judge you for your wildness or forlornness or even your beauty. In a world where everyone is striving for perfection and alikeness, anyone who follows an unpaved pathway is deemed abnormal."

He took a bite .I nodded although I didn't quite understand a lot of what he was saying. Kids were mean to me, I wanted it to stop, end off.

"Amy, sweetie; I don't want you to change to adapt to their degrading standards. I want you to wake up each morning happy with where you are but most importantly happy with who you are. London is a big city Amy and there are millions of people to be friends with but there's also a world out there that is so much bigger than London, I promise one day you will love it. But until that day comes we are not going to sit on our backside and let these kids get away with being immature prats."

I smiled. We finished our cupcakes and stood up to go.

"So I've decided, we're moving."

I'd never loved anyone so much as I did my dad in that moment. I squeezed him as hard as we could and when we got back in the car we drove a long roundabout way home. We passed dozens of houses for sale, including the one we live in today.

Chapter 5

Tara wasn't in school on Monday. I had text her, rung her, even her house phone but her mum said she wasn't ready yet, she then progressed to whisper for me to come over tomorrow.

"Where's Tara?" asked Lily in assembly, "Sam was asking for her this morning, but she's been MIA since Friday night, she totally gave him the cold shoulder. You've been MIA too Amy, how was your weekend?"

I walked back to class with Lily, telling her it was fine, that Mike needed my help with a project.

"I miss you Amy," she said suddenly, "you and Tara too, I feel like we're losing our squadness, gosh that sounds silly." She smiled but I could see she was genuinely upset. I'd been so worried these past few weeks I'd forgotten to be a good friend to almost everyone. I hugged her.

"I know what you mean, but hey let's have a sleepover just us three next weekend. It'll be like old times."

That made her smile and she sat down beside me in English. "I'm going to write a list of all the things we can discuss and do," she whispered. I smiled back. She really was the sweetest girl. I thought of when we first met, it was here in English class when I was new. Lily had this big bunch of friends but she still was so kind to me. I was overwhelmed after years of cruelty, to find someone like Lily. Soon she started to sit with Tara and I and things just kind of clicked. She always organised exciting things to do at the weekend and she would randomly bring us in chocolates or socks or something for the most bizarre occasions. Like on 'world nutella day' she bought us each a heart shaped jar of nutella and when we went to hers later that night she had cooked us piles of pancakes. She showered us all in so much love. I don't know how you'd describe Lily in a few words but all I can honestly say is she's just a really amazing friend.

Lily wanted to go for coffee after school but I bid her a hasty goodbye, saying I was late to the dentist. I caught the bus over to Dr Foster's. I had told Mum this morning I wanted to go alone, she protested at first but then I think she was just as scared as I was. Neither of us knew what the boundaries were in this situation so she agreed. I'm almost 100% sure she rang Dr Foster after I left for school. I just didn't want Mum there for what I was about to say.

Dr Foster had gone to the reception to get some lab results. I sat nervously in her room, wringing my hands in front of me.

"I want an abortion," I blurted out as soon as she walked back into the room.

"You do?" she asked.

I nodded quickly.

"Okay," Dr Foster sat down at her desk and began typing. Just like that. I was slightly in shock but maybe this happened almost every day, maybe I wasn't such a minority after all.

"Now, from your blood results we're able to confirm that you are about six weeks along so I would say a month from now to carry out the termination."

Termination; god I knew that was what they called it but it seemed so harsh, so final. I felt sick. I was already six weeks pregnant. My mind reeled but it made sense. Luke and I had been going out two years on New Years.

"Okay, ehm, what do I do then?" I asked.

"Well a month from now puts us on March 15th. Is that an okay date for you to have the procedure?"

Dr Foster must have seen my pale face and shaking hands.

"This isn't your only option Amy, but if you feel like it's what is best for you then we are to give you all the support you need."

I nodded, taking it all in.

"There's a clinic, no that's a bad word for it; there's a place over near Islington. It's kind of a women's run place for young women who are either pregnant or have young children themselves. The people are really lovely and they meet three times a week, there will be girls there in your situation and ones who have gone through what you may do yourself. I'd really advise giving them a visit one evening Amy. I'll call and tell the lady there to expect one of my patients okay?"

I said yes, thinking no way on earth was I heading all the way over there to feel awkward amongst a group of girls who led completely different lives to me.

"Okay, great." She smiled brightly, "Now that's all for today, we'll call to arrange another appointment before the procedure just to go through everything involved."

"Great, thanks so much Dr," I said, hopping off the leather bed and making my way towards the door.

"Amy," said Dr Foster.

"Your very brave, just remember; it's a long life, " she smiled. I nodded and let myself out. It's a long life I thought as I began walking towards Tara's; but we only have one so I'd better make Tara believe in hers before it was too late.

She was on her couch, watching re runs of 'Grey's Anatomy' our joint favourite show.

"Oh no, Izzy dies in this episode," I said sitting down next to her.

"Shh, it's about to happen," whispered Tara, holding the blanket up to her, she threw one over me. I wrapped it around myself as we watched the scene unfold.

When the credits started I looked over to Tara and a silent tear was gliding down her cheek.

"It'll be okay Tara, I promise."

"I'm so disappointed in myself," she said quietly. "I never thought I'd let it get that far…"

"How long?" I asked, scared of the answer.

"Since September really… It sounds so stupid but I wanted to keep those summer bodies we'd worked so hard for, remember all the runs and karate classes."

We both laughed, they had been a flunk.

"Tara you don't need to do that to yourself."

"I know, of course I know that but then with all the stress and…" she whispered. "Mum and Dad on my back about medicine it just seemed like the one thing I could control in my life while they were trying to take control of my future. Oh Amy I'm so embarrassed, but I've to go to this place now every Wednesday evening, I really don't want to but Mum and Dad are so afraid I'll start again."

"Have you stopped?" I asked

Tara nodded, "I'm trying to… I mean it's only been a few days and I've gone that long before but just eating and everything is hard. That's why I didn't go to school. I can't bear the thought of the canteen and then having to …." Her voice trailed off.

"No, you won't have to I promise. You're going to get better Tara; you are like the strongest person I know. Please go to the place on Wednesday and please come to school tomorrow, no-one else need ever know."

"That's exactly what I want Amy, nobody to know, please don't tell Lily she would worry so much and then she would probably bake me a cake or something and that would really just top it all off."

We laughed, because that's what best friends do, we laugh at the difficult things to make them that bit easier.

"Don't worry, everything is going to okay, what do we always say?" I asked cheerfully.

Tara smiled. "Everything…" I joined in with her, "always happens for a reason."

I wasn't sure I believed those words anymore. Maybe some things just happen and we have no control. Or if they do, I wish to god I knew what the reasons were.

Chapter 6

A week later I was sitting on a bus. Life was strangely normal. Tara was back in school, I could see her struggle sometimes but Lily was doing a good job of cheering her up. Even if Lily didn't actually know what was going on with Tara, I knew she sensed something had happened. She didn't ask questions, she just helped. She was good like that. We hadn't had our pre-planned sleepover these past two weekends but I knew Tara wasn't ready for popcorn and cupcakes and well I wasn't ready for confined space with the two people I told everything to. Luke and I, well we were talking about everything. I hadn't yet told him I'd already a date for an abortion. I think that's why I was on this bus, to figure out how to do the rest.

I got off the bus at the Highgate and Islington stop. I was rarely in this part of the city, and I was rarely catching buses around London after school alone. But I was at my wits end and the booklet that Dr Foster had given me during our last consultation seemed to be as good a shot as any at figuring out where to go from here. I followed the little map on the back of the booklet until I was standing outside what appeared to be an old renovated church. A woman with a double buggy was struggling to get through the tall, narrow doors and a girl no older than Mike tried to help her. Both of the girl's stomach looked ready to burst. I took a few steps forward and followed the two girls into the building. Once inside I started to panic. I saw a group of three other pregnant girls surrounded by toddlers aching for their attention. My chest tightened. I mean I knew this place was going to be full of young mothers but I hadn't expected it to seem so, so real. I turned to leave. A firm hand took my shoulder.

"Hello there darling, are you our lovely newbie?" drawled a South African lady, dressed head to toe in colourful garments. I envied her bravery of style for a moment. Her eyes were old and wrinkled but her smile was young and vibrant, taking at least ten years off her actual age I guessed.

"I, um I'm…" I started, what was wrong with me. Speak. She put her arm around my shoulder in a motherly way.

"Now don't be worried. I can see how walking into this loud mess can be a bit overwhelming but once you settle in I'm sure you'll consider this your second home. Remember, this is a place you can come and feel completely non-judged."

I nodded and she smiled; unwrapping her arm from behind me she clapped her hands together to get all of the girl's attention. There wasn't a boy in sight, apart from a few toddlers maybe.

"Alright everyone, time to head into the main hall and take a seat."

I followed the group as we made our way further into the old building, coming into a snug room with about fifteen chairs set up in a circle. In the corner there was a soft mat spread out with a collection of toys laid out. Everyone took a seat, until I and another girl with long but dead looking light brown hair were the only two standing.

"Ah Crystal! Your back, I thought you had left us for good," cried the lady in the colourful garments. "Take a seat you two."

The girl who I now knew was Crystal looked at me and smiled. "Come on," she mouthed and took my hand, leading me to two spare sits in the circle. Crystal was very pregnant and she wore a bright pink top that didn't fully cover her bump. Her dirty tracksuit bottoms had holes in them. If I had seen Crystal under any other circumstances; I would have avoided eye contact and possibly crossed to the other side of the road. Now I was ashamed to think I would have even considered that. Once seated she let go of my hand.

"Great girls, now we have a new lovely lady today. Gosh and I haven't even introduced myself to her yet, well I'm Deborah and I lead this group every second day. Now love; introduce yourself to the group and tell us a few words about yourself. Why you're here and how you're feeling etc. Then we will all tell you our little stories okay?"

I nodded. I could see Crystal smiling encouragingly at me.

"I'm Amy," I said. "Ehm, I'm 17 and I guess I'm here because, well I'm pregnant."

The whole group laughed and I didn't feel like such an alien.

"Great work Amy, well I'm Deborah. When I was fifteen I got pregnant because of rape. I had my baby, a gorgeous little girl who I named Zara but she died of cot death at only three weeks old. When I finished school I decided I wanted to help women who needed the help I needed so badly when I was young, so here we are today. Now girls, you know the drill."

A young girl with a baby on her lap sitting next to Deborah started talking. She was nineteen and her baby was now four months old. She got pregnant after having sex for the first time at a party with a boy she barely knew. She never told the boy.

The next girl grew up in foster care and had been sexually abused by the people who were supposed to be looking after her one weekend. She was now seven months pregnant and living with a new family whom she said she adored. She said she was going to give the baby up for adoption once it was born.

The girl's stories continued, each one as sad, shocking but somewhat amazing as the other. I admired all these girls who I would have once labelled a bunch of unsightly names.

The next girl spoke, her name was Katie. She was twenty and she wanted to have an abortion. "I haven't told anyone in my family yet, but the father of the baby wants me to and I think I do too."

"Remember Katie, it's your body and your choice," said Deborah.

"I know," sighed Katie, "but is it awful that it's what I want too?"

I exhaled. *Someone I could really relate to*, I thought.

"It's not awful at all," perked up a blonde haired girl a few seats to my left. "I had an abortion two weeks ago and I'm twenty-one but no way am I ready to be a mother. It wouldn't be right for me, or for the baby. One in three women will have an abortion in their life. It doesn't need to be looked upon so harshly in my opinion. Do what you feel you want Katie," she then smiled at me, "I'm Sandra by the way."

I nodded and then spoke. "I think I'm going to get an abortion too," I said looking down at my hands. "I feel I'm too young and I won't be any good to a new child."

Crystal moved in her seat next to me.

"I understand your choices completely Katie and Amy and I one hundred percent agree that it is the woman's choice and it is not a bad thing at all. But I couldn't imagine giving up my little girl. I don't know why but I can't wait to be her mum but girls I know exactly how you feel and respect you so much for doing what you feel is right. After all it's different for everyone," Crystal smiled and shrugged and I smiled back.

"Lovely words Crystal," said Deborah. "Now everyone, what do you think is the most misjudged thing people think about young pregnant women?"

This got all the girls talking passionately and loudly. I sat back quiet and listened to everything they said. They were so wise for being so young. Maybe pregnancy did that to you. And they were right too; lots of people would think they were sluts, or part time druggies. I knew this because only a few weeks ago, although I rarely thought of it, they may have been my thoughts too.

"I think it's insane because it's like somehow we got ourselves pregnant. We get all the dirty looks and the pursed lips. It's like no, we didn't just wind up like this ourselves. There was a boy involved and he walks away unscathed. It's insanely wrong," said the girl who grew up in foster care. Carla was her name.

Deborah wound the session up a couple of minutes later and everyone got up to leave chattering away as they did. I walked out into the fresh air.

"Hey, hey Amy wait up," shouted a voice behind me. I spun around and Crystal was moving slowly, her hand resting on her protruding stomach.

"Wanna talk a quick walk? Grab a Starbuck's, I think this baby needs some sugar it's kicking like a mad woman," she laughed.

I looked at her stomach, the sight of it alien to me. "Here, have a feel." She grabbed my hand and placed it on her warm stomach. I thought I would hate this but I could feel what felt like millions of little butterflies inside her. I smiled.

"Starbucks?" she asked, starting to walk. I hate to admit this, but I hesitated. Not because I was worried my mum would wonder where I was or because I didn't want to get the bus home in the dark. I hesitated because, as horrible and awful as this sounds, a part of me didn't want to be associated with a dirty looking young pregnant girl. Some terrible part of my mind screamed, think of who you are, think of your reputation.

"Are you coming?" asked Crystal, smiling so wide and happy. *Screw that*, I thought, *that was then. I'm not that person anymore.* "Coming," I said running after her.

My Reputation

It wasn't until I moved school that I got a 'solid, don't mess with her' one. Before that as you know I was the weirdo, the freak and that hurt me so much that anything would be better. Tara had a reputation. Her reputation was doing whatever she wanted whenever she wanted and although not many people were friends with her, those who were loved her without hesitation. My reputation wasn't like that at all. I guess mine was more given to me. My reputation came along with Luke, he was the first one who noticed me and once we were together I became more noticed. Not for bad reasons, Luke was a good-looking boy but by no means was he a player. I was his first girlfriend and apparently everyone who knew him all his life had bets on who it would be, seeing as most of the boys at this stage had already been associated with someone, he was different in that sense. I was fresh meat and no one ever suspected it would be me. The fact that he had never showed any interest in other girls, beyond the occasional kiss on a night out, could have given the girls reason to hate me; but then the fact that I had befriended Lily who was friends on a low level basis with everyone and the fact that I was already known as Tara's best friend stopped that too. High school was complicated. So they didn't hate me, instead they respected me. Instead people actually saw me and they liked me and everyone thought I was one of the nicest girls in our year. I'm not saying this to sound conceited, I'm saying it because it's true. Sure I didn't actively know most of them on a personal level, but it's harder to remain liking someone if you do. Maybe that's why they all liked me, they didn't know me. So thus my reputation was born. I was the nice girl, the good girl with the lovely family, the cute boyfriend and rock solid best friends. I didn't do anything out of the ordinary, that wasn't who I was. I trotted along every day, saying hellos and goodbyes and smiling and everyone was happy. We all have a reputation; we all have a person we're expected to be. This was mine.

Chapter 7

Over the next week, I met Crystal almost every day. I told Mum I was going to the clinic Dr Foster had suggested and she respected that. Dad still wasn't happy with me but he at least wished me a good day after breakfast each morning. I was avoiding Luke like the plague for some reason my mind hadn't yet comprehended, I knew it wasn't good but he was caught up in assignments at the moment and wanted to get everything done before worrying.

Crystal just got it, and she was funny and kind and so brave. I felt like I could talk to her about all my thoughts and even though she was dead set on keeping her little girl, she didn't judge me for what I wanted to do.

"So it's my uncle that got me pregnant," she shared on our fourth day of meeting. Even though neither of us lived near the Starbucks in Islington, we continued to meet here. It felt like a safe place for both of us.

I almost choked on my caramel hot chocolate.

She nodded. "I know it's…"

Tears were forming in her eyes but she quickly wiped them away. I'd never seen her cry before and in the short week we'd known each other we'd covered a wide range of topics; many of which had me puffy cheeked and red eyed; but Crystal was strong; I reached out and took her hand.

"I don't see him anymore, my dad found out and he almost killed him on the street. He left and I don't know where he went. I don't want to know."

"Did you never tell?" I asked, concerned.

"It only happened twice, once when I was very young. At our Christmas party, I was twelve maybe. My mum, well," Crystal took a deep breath, "she's not in the picture so I was always with my dad and his brothers. We played cards and stuff, they were fun to be around until…"

I could barely bare to hear this but I somehow felt it was important to Crystal that she told me.

"Until Uncle Rob started doing stuff at that Christmas party when everyone else was too drunk to notice. I was too scared to say anything afterwards and because he never tried anything again I stayed silent. Then six months ago…" Her voice trailed off and she looked up to the sky. Her voice shook; "I told my dad that time."

"Oh god Crystal, that is awful I am so, so sorry."

"But it's okay Amy, really because it gave me Bella." Bella was what she was going to call her daughter, although I was still unsure about how she indented to raise her.

"I have an aunt, my mum's sister and she told me if I ever get in trouble I can go and be with her. She was the kindest lady I'd ever met. She made me chocolate chip cookies as a kid. She lives in the country now I think, I sent her an email, she'll get back to me soon and when Bella's born, the two of us can go be with her. It'll be a whole new beginning for me Amy!" Crystal looked so happy, so content. I couldn't say a thing. I doubted this aunt's reliability and I worried for both Crystal and Bella's future, but there was nothing I could do. I just smiled and thanked whatever god there was that I lived the life I did; no matter what. That night I hugged all of my family extra tight before going to bed. Especially Mike.

"You're the best ever okay," I whispered into his rock solid gelled hair.

"You're a weirdo," he said pushing me away but he smiled as I left, "Glad to see you back to yourself sis, you'll be okay."

Chapter 8
March

I took a deep breath as I rang the 'oh so familiar' doorbell. I was more nervous than I'd anticipated. It was my first time to go to Luke's since the whole pregnancy had come out. He had told his parents soon enough afterwards, their reaction had been much like my dad's. Not good. But apparently now they were completely okay with it. I found this hard to believe. I hadn't seen them since but Luke had told me to come over this evening in an attempt to break the ice. I still hadn't told him about the abortion. Mom and Dad were both oblivious too. I was going to tell them tonight; March 15th was only four days away.

Luke's sister opened the door. She was a few years older than us and in college on the south side of the city.

"Hi," I said, smiling.

Kathy rolled her eyes and turned around. "She's here," she shouted, walking away from me. I let myself in and closed the door quietly behind me. That was colder than I'd expected from her. She was the one who used to help sneak me in and out of Luke's room in the early days. Luke appeared at the end of the hall, he pulled me in to a hug. I guessed his parents couldn't see us so I hugged him back tightly. It had been too long since I'd felt this safe.

"I've missed you so much Amy, I'm sorry I've been so caught up in schoolwork but I've gotten everything in now, we can concentrate on you and me and well all of this." He kissed my forehead like he always did and led me into the kitchen.

His mum was sitting at the table reading a book, she was a lecturer of philosophy in Kings College and she was always reading, what I don't really know; but she had a lot of wise things to say at dinnertime whenever I was there. Sometimes she'd ask us these questions that had no real proper answer, they used to make me feel awkward but now I often looked forward to them when I came here; I could see it was where Luke got his deep thinking side from and I loved that. Luke's dad was standing over the cooker, on his phone. He ran some sort of computer company and was extremely efficient and practical, the complete opposite of Luke's mum but I guess sometimes opposites attract, or at least they say so.

"Amy, hello, how are you?" asked Luke's mum, Sandy was her name, "have a seat."

"I'm good thanks, you?" I asked, sitting down across from her, Luke sat next to me.

"Amy," greeted his dad, Tim, turning off his phone and sitting down next to his wife. It felt like an interrogation. I looked at Luke; he could see the discomfort in my face.

"Ehm Mum…" he was at a loss of words.

"Oh my gosh, look at me," cried his mum jumping up, her long violet cardigan sweeping the floor. "I had baked us all some rocky road cause I know you just love it Amy." I smiled. Tim rolled his eyes but looked relieved at the distraction. Bringing out baked goods in the middle of what was probably going to be a very serious situation didn't really seem suitable but any kind of distraction would do. While Sandy took out the rocky road, Tim asked me how school was going and we talked about Luke upcoming exams for getting into Edinburgh, he wanted to study Law and Philosophy there, *a good mix for him*, I thought.

"Now here we are," Sandy laid out plates and delicious looking rocky road. We all dug in, the ice broken.

"So Amy, how is everything going with the pregnancy? Let's not dance about the truth," asked Tim. I didn't really want him here to be honest but how did I say that now without sounding rude.

"Ehm well," I started, my face going red because well pregnancy equals because of sex and I didn't like to think about what they could be thinking.

'Tim, honestly, you have such a lack of awareness, why don't you just go for a little while and me and Amy can talk about this okay,' said Sandy, smiling at me and swatting Tim away, although I sometimes found Tim intimidating, I liked their relationship. Tim rolled his eyes and took his rocky road with him, patting Luke on the back on his way out.

With Tim gone, I started to talk.

"Look, I don't know how you," I turned to Luke, "or your family will feel about this but I think I've decided what I'm going to do.'

Sandy's face went white and Luke grabbed my hand.

"But Amy, we haven't really talked yet," he said.

"I know, I know," I replied, "but I am booked to have an abortion on the 15th."

Sandy looked at me, "Oh Amy!"

Luke let go of my hand. "Amy I wanted us to talk about this at least, look that gives us no time."

'Luke, look I know but it's what's best for me and for you, what can we do for a baby Luke honestly."

"I don't know Amy but this just seems like a rash decision, I don't know, it's killing a life."

I was speechless for a moment. "No, it's not Luke, look one in three women will have an abortion in their life," I said thinking of my first session at the group. "It's not such a big deal if we don't make it one okay, I'm going to tell Mum and Dad tonight."

"You haven't told them yet? Amy honestly!" he paused, "But one in three, really?"

"Crazy right?" I said, all of the ice gone out of our voices.

"Wow, yeah…"

"I've been going to this young women's group, we all sit around and talk about our options and thoughts and stuff and it's really helped me to get a clearer head, and I've made a friend, Crystal, god she's so lovely but her story's so sad Luke I've got to tell you sometime."

"What? Since when have you been going here Amy you haven't told me any of this! I feel like you're just cutting me off at a time when we really need each other." He shook his head and looked down, he was right, I had cut him off. He turned to me.

"Okay Amy, of course I support whatever decision you make, I'm sorry I know abortion isn't like… what I said it was. I'm sorry," he took my hand, "but you don't need to cut me out okay, I'm not going to leave just because things get rough, let me help you make decisions okay. You're not all alone in this." I nodded, my eyes watering.

Sandy sniffed, I had forgotten she was there, I think Luke had too, we both turned to face her.

"Well in all my years," she said, smiling. "I don't know why they give out about the young; you two are much wiser than I ever was at your age." She stood up.

"You're going to be just fine Amy," she smiled at me, taking my hand before leaving the kitchen.

"That went well," laughed Luke. I nodded, my eyes wide.

"I'm just glad they didn't ask about the how's," I said, "that was all my dad's mind seemed to be doing, he chose to be insanely naïve I think." I laughed.

"Even after that time?" asked Luke, smiling at the memory.

"Oh no," I cried, my face going red just thinking about it. "He has definitely permanently erased that from his mind," I laughed.

"I hope," said Luke and I unison before laughing.

The First Time (Or That Time)

It was January, we were both sixteen and had been together for just over a year. Luke was over at my house on a Friday night and we were on the couch watching Twilight of all movies and laughing at the cringiness of the whole film.

"I think if I ever woke up and thought I saw you watching me sleep from my window I'd move country, not fall deeper in love with you," I laughed.

"I don't think I'd blame you."

"Promise to never turn into a vampire and do creepy stuff like that," I smiled, holding out my pinky.

"I swear," he said latching his finger into mine before using it to pull me on top of him. I laughed and kissed him. The movie played on in the background.

"Let's go upstairs," I said, after a few minutes. I'm not sure why I thought that moment was a good one or how I knew I was ready; but I just did and upstairs we went. Tripping over ourselves as we hurried up the two flights, Mike was at a sleepover and my parents were still at work. We both knew what was about to happen. I was nervous but I was ready, and at this stage I didn't trust anyone in the world more than I trusted Luke.

Afterwards, we both lay there beside each other for a while, the air around us seemed to have shifted and I felt closer to him than I ever had before; we talked about everything. But I won't lie, a lot of my mind space was being taken up with how frikkin' sore it was and why had no one told me it was that painful, thanks. Then I heard a faint buzzing sound.

"Shh," I said to Luke, propping up on my elbow and putting my finger to his lips.

He moved up as if to listen, and there it was; a ringing.

"My phone!" I said, "I left it downstairs, shit what if it's Mike or something, he always claims feeling sick at sleepovers."

Luke laughed, "I'll run down and get it," he said hopping out of bed and pulling on his boxers, he was looking to throw on his pants too but the ringing was still going.

"Just be quick, don't worry no one will see you," I said. He nodded and ran out of the room, leaving the door open behind him. A minute later the ringing stopped, I guessed Luke must have got it.

"Great," I shouted down to him, "Now come back up here, I'm getting cold without you," I yelled just as I heard the front door slam. I sat up in a panic.

"Luke?" I heard my dad's voice say in confusion; shit, shit, shit, was all I could think. I jumped out of bed, pulled on the red dressing gown lying on my ground and raced down the stairs. My dad was standing just inside the doorway and directly in front of him just having stepped out of the living room was Luke, in his underwear; my pink iPhone in hand. It almost looked worse than it actually was; which is saying a lot because it was already pretty bad. Luke's mouth was open but nothing was coming out.

"Dad," I blurted out, from the bottom of the stairs. He turned around to see me in my dressing gown. It wasn't one he'd ever seen before, it was red and silky and the girls had got it for me for Christmas, handed to me with a wink from Tara.

"Amy," he said, I could see his mind racing to think of any reasons we were both like this, other than the obvious.

"Luke just got here from training," I said, "He was all sweaty and I told him he could have a shower, that's okay right?" I said, smiling sweetly. Dad nodded slowly, looking over at Luke who was nodding in agreement. "Yeah, ehm really terrible weather tonight…"

Dad looked back to me. I could see he wanted to question my outfit choice. I tried to be as blasé as possible, "Oh me? Oh I was just about to hop into bed, I'm dead after this week but then of course Luke did one of his surprise visits."

"Yeah sorry Mr Webb," said Luke, "and I was just getting Amy's phone to call my mum to come and get me." There was a silence.

"Mine died," Luke said to break it. I almost laughed out loud but redeemed myself.

"Oh yes okay, well ehm, I was just popping back to pick up a fresh pair of clothes; I've got to work a night shift tonight Amy," he looked from me to Luke, then back to me, "But your mum will be home soon, no doubt."

"Okay great Dad, Luke will just get his stuff together. I'll see you in the morning." I smiled cheerily, looking intently at Luke to follow me back upstairs. He did some kind of an awkward wave to my dad before running up after me. In my room we silently freaked out until the front door slammed shut again. We laughed then freaked out then laughed some more.

My dad has never mentioned the moment to me ever. Even the next morning I tried to explain it better to him. He just looked at me and said, "Amy, Luke needed to shower, you don't need to reassure me; I know you'd never be that silly."

"Yeah I'd never be that silly."

I left Luke's that night with what felt like a weight off my shoulders, he was okay, we were okay; what I was doing was okay.

I let myself in at home,

"Family meeting," I called out more joyously than I'd probably sounded in weeks. Sometimes it felt like I was watching myself play the blasé funny young girl on a TV sitcom that people watched when they wanted to zone out. What had happened to me?

Mike came down the stairs, followed by Dad, both looking suspiciously at me. Maybe Dad's face wasn't suspicious maybe it was more petrified but I was feeling optimistic so let's say it looked positive. Mum came out of the kitchen.

"You sound happy," she said, smiling at me. Dad looked at her disapprovingly. I knew they'd been fighting over how they should be handling the situation. It made me feel awful and I wanted it to end. This would end it all right. The word 'terminate' popped into my head again; I tried to wipe it away.

I brought them all into the living room and sat down across from them.

"Okay; I know I've made a mistake, or well you know, whatever were going to call this," Mike laughed and Dad whacked his knee. "Ow," he cried out pathetically.

"This is serious, Mike, quit it," said Dad.

"Okay," I continued, taking a deep breath, "we don't need to drag this out any further; I've decided to have an abortion and I have an appointment to get on the 15th."

"Whoa!" said Mike.

"Oh Amy good girl, you've made a wise choice," said Dad, smiling at me for the first time since February.

"Jacob stop," said Mum. "Amy hold on a minute; are you sure this is what you want? Don't feel like, because of your situation or age or anything that you have to. You very well could regret this."

"Liz, what are you talking about, why would she regret it? This is her only option. She's not being a teen mother for god's sake."

"You don't need to say it like that, these things happen okay. We're not going to be the parents who disown their daughter or force her into things okay and you've been acting like an awful father look at yourself."

"That's enough Liz," Dad raised his voice. "Amy's getting an abortion and that's that!"

"Amy," I said loudly, "is right here." They both went silent, "and please stop fighting about me. I know what I'm going to do and thank you, Mum, for all your support; and Dad, well, I don't even know what you think of me anymore but thanks for making it very clear how you would feel if I were to god forbid be a 'teen mom' and with that I got up and stormed out of the room. I pounded up the stairs but then I heard footsteps behind me.

"Amy wait," said Mike. I turned around.

"I found a new place yesterday," he said smiling, "do you want to see the pictures?"

I was about to burst into tears but I nodded and we both walked into his room.

I stayed in there with Mike until late, when I went to bed I was too worn out to think and I feel fast asleep. When I woke up the next morning I had over twenty missed calls. All from Crystal's number and then one single message from an unknown number 'Amy, try get to the hospital quick; Crystal needs you. Deborah x'

Chapter 9

I was sitting in the hospital waiting room for the second time in what felt like far too short of time. When I raced out the door that morning an hour before school, Mum and Dad both looked worried about me; but there was no time to explain who Crystal was and how in the space of a week or two she had become so important to me.

"Amy, you're here!" said a strong loud, voice, Deborah of course. She came over and sat next to me.

"Oh no what's happened?" I asked, taking in her fatigued face and sad eyes.

"Crystal's lost her baby," said Deborah softly, in almost a whisper.

"But how?" I asked. "What happened?"

Deborah shook her head sadly. "It's hard to know in the circumstances sometimes Amy, but she just miscarried in the early hours of this morning. She's heartbroken."

I was lost for words. That baby was Crystal's lifeline. It was all that gave her hope in this world. It was her way out.

"The only other person she wanted to see was you Amy; Crystal doesn't have many friends. That's why she stopped coming to our sessions for so long before you joined. She likes you though, no she really loves you."

I nodded, a tear falling from my eye. *Poor Crystal;* I thought, *poor lost Crystal*. And I almost didn't give her a chance, on that very first day we meet; I almost said no and left her alone for fear of stepping outside of what I had always known.

"It's strange isn't it Deborah," I said suddenly, my mind racing.

"What is sweetie?" she asked, looking confused.

"The way one word, or one small decision; can change the whole course of your life, can even shape who you become. If I hadn't gone for coffee with Crystal when she first asked me; I would never have known that people aren't as black or white as they appear to be. I wouldn't have thought outside my own box and I wouldn't be sitting her right now. It's almost as if we're all just walking blindly, and the further we go, the more we see."

Deborah smiled. "You're right Amy, the paths of our lives do lie in circumstance; in choice and luck and chance. Maybe we should talk about it in our next session; but what I need you to do right now is, go in there and talk to that new friend of yours. You don't need to say much, just enough for her to know you're here okay."

"Of course." I nodded and I followed her down the hall.

Crystal's pale face was propped up by two big white pillows. She looked so little in the bed. My eyes automatically flew to where her massive stomach had once been. There was still a bump but it was tiny in comparison. My stomach tightened.

"Hey there," I said softly, sitting down in the seat next to her. She turned her head to face me.

"I can't cry anymore, I think I've lost all my tears," she said steadily.

I took her hand. "Crystal I'm so sorry."

She looked straight ahead, "I've nothing now Amy; nothing."

"You've me," I said.

"Being pregnant was the only reason we were friends in the first place."

"That doesn't matter now," I said quietly.

"Of course it does; our lives are different. Mine's messy, I'm messy, you're good, you'll do good things. The best thing I could do with my life was convince myself that being pregnant was good for me. Who was I kidding; I was never going to hear back from my aunt."

"You don't know that," I said, "but Crystal it's okay. We'll figure out what you can do, we will make it work." I didn't know how I was going to save Crystal from her life but I couldn't just say nothing.

"No, you don't have to do anything. I'm fine, my dad will probably be happy at least." She burst into tears. They can keep coming no matter how hard you've cried.

She continued, "Knowing him he'll tell my uncle everything is okay now and he'll come back. He always preferred them to me anyways."

"No Crystal we can't let that happen; please let me help you," I pleaded.

Her eyes suddenly glazed over, she looked at me. "You've helped me enough Amy, thank you so much. I think I need to sleep now."

I squeezed her hand, wanting to say more but not knowing anything that would help her in any way.

"Please call me, and I'll see you soon okay."

Crystal just nodded and closed her eyes. I let myself out.

Obviously, I couldn't concentrate in school that day.

"You okay?" asked Tara after I answered wrong to our math's teacher for the third time that class.

"Yeah; just super tired," I said, forcing a smile.

"What about you?" I then asked her when the bell rang, "How's everything?"

"Oh good," she said quietly, "the… Wednesday's we'll call them… they're really helping."

Lily came up behind us in the hall. "Hello ladies." She smiled and then pointed her finger at Tara, "you little missy, need to talk to Sam."

Tara sighed loudly but Lily put up her hand. "Look he's been on my case for months; what is going on with you two?"

"I just really don't have time for any boy drama right now," said Tara.

"Amy's got a boyfriend," said Lily, "she's fine! And me well, you know I just like to float." She laughed at herself, "but honestly Amy, he's really into you and you used to be crazy about him; what happened?"

Lily was right, for years our brave Tara had held onto a 'long time' crush on a cute boy in our group called Sam. Only a few months ago he started talking to Luke about how he thought she was cute, they talked a bit, I thought things might actually go somewhere for them.

"I just, I," started Tara but just then Luke walked over to us.

"Hey Amy, hey girls," he said smiling at them, "can I talk to you for a minute?" He said to me. I nodded and we stepped back away from the girls who were now being joined by some of Luke's friends.

"I want to come with you on Wednesday yeah?" he said softly, ensuring no one would hear. *Wednesday, Wednesday*; I thought; my mind racing. With everything that happened with Crystal my mind had thought of nothing else.

"The 15th, the day," said Luke; looking at me worryingly.

"Oh god yeah of course; sorry complete mind blank there. Yes please do," I said.

"Of course," he said smiling. "It's in the morning right? I'll meet you at the station, just text me a time."

I nodded; Tara and Lily had walked back over within hearing distance of us.

"Ooh the two of you running off for a date day, ye are shocking," laughed Lily.

"With exams right around the corner too, see this is why I definitely don't need a boyfriend," joked Tara and both her and Lily laughed. Sam had followed them and heard what Lily said; he looked deflated. I widened my eyes at Tara to signal that Sam was behind her, she spun around.

"Oh hey Sam, oh you know ehm," her voice trailed off and he walked away. Luke and I looked at each other. Usual teenage life carried on was what we both were thinking and I knew we both wished it was what our heads were most caught up in at the moment.

Chapter 10

It was early Wednesday morning and I was waiting outside the Lua Tube for Luke. Mum, Dad and I had all talked lots about my decision last night and we all thought it was for the best; even Mum. She had said something along the lines of 'it wouldn't stay with me as much' I didn't really understand. They agreed to let me just go with Luke; it was our thing now. Though I knew Mum wished she were with me, I kind of wished she were too but I was trying to be brave, for her, for Luke, for me I guess. I had text her twice already though.

I hadn't heard from Crystal yet and it was bothering me, I had gone to the group last night and she wasn't there. I realised I didn't even know where she lived.

"Hello," said Luke sneaking up behind me, "how you feeling?"

I nodded and took a breath. "I'm good, I'm good. I'm ready," I said, but there was something niggling at the back of my head. I couldn't quite place it but it had been there ever since Monday and it was driving me crazy.

We caught the tube towards Redbridge, this is where the clinic was; it was a part of the King Georges hospital but a part I'd never been to before obviously.

When we walked up the steps to the entrance I started to feel really sick. Luke took my hand. "It's okay Amy, you'll be fine; I promise." He looked me straight in the eyes and I trusted him. We walked in the doors and were seated in a waiting room. Surrounded by women of all ages my head started to spin. I rested it on Luke's shoulder. *No, there was definitely something wrong*, I thought. It was that niggling; whatever it was at the back of my mind that was bothering me.

"Luke," I started to say just as a nurse walked over to us. She smiled. "Amy Webb, would you follow me please?"

I looked at Luke; he looked at me. I looked at all of the women surrounding me; their eyes stood out and I thought of Crystal.

"No," I said; I'm not sure who to; the nurse maybe, Luke, me?

"No," I repeated; thinking of the eyes. Thinking of Crystal's eyes and how they glazed over, how she had given up in that moment and how she would never be the same again.

"Amy what's wrong?" asked Luke gently.

"I can't do it," I said, looking at him. I couldn't explain the Crystal story to him; it wouldn't make sense. I didn't understand it myself but right now it felt intensely right to not go through with the abortion.

"Okay," he said slowly; not knowing what to do.

The nurse spoke, "Don't worry Amy, a lot of people are torn making this decision. We have people here you can talk to if you would like?"

I shook my head and stood up. Luke stood up quickly with me. "No," I said, "thank you though; but I know what I want to do. Sorry for taking up your time." I grabbed Luke's hand and started walking back out. Once in the fresh air; we stopped and we looked at each other. Luke smiled, I smiled. To this day I can't explain how right that decision felt but it just did.

"We can do this," he said and I nodded. "Come on; let's go on a mystery tour."

Luke led me on to the tube; of course not letting me see which direction we were going in. He did love his mystery tours; he'd done a few with me over our years, they always marked significant chapters in our lives.

"Where are you taking me this time?" I mockingly whined as we sat down in the tube.

"Somewhere new," he said; tapping away on his phone. "You're going to love it." I felt free and young again; running around the city like this with Luke.

"But first we may need to stop for some clothes," he grinned at me.

"What why?" I asked, puzzled. "Well I can't tell you silly but you are going to need a dress and I am going to need some nicer trousers and definitely some kind of blazer."

The tube stopped and Luke got up. "This is us," he said and we walked out.

"Luke, why do I need a dress? I'm not marrying you, you know," I joked.

"Oh what a good idea…" his voice trailed off and I widened my eyes, "kidding," he laughed, "no, not a white dress. Any colour will do, here let's try this charity shop; we don't have much cash." We were standing outside a blue painted charity shop.

"Sounds good to me," I said, "but wait, I'm going to turn off my phone for the day."

"Good idea," agreed Luke. Turning off his 'let's just escape for a little while'.

I nodded in agreement and together we walked into the shop.

When we came out half an hour later we were two completely different people. I interlocked my arm into Luke's and we strolled along the street. I was wearing a rose gold halter necked dress with long, dangly, expensive looking earrings (they had cost two pounds.) On my feet there was a pair of gold small-heeled sandals. My toes were numb but I didn't care. Luke next to me was in navy suit trousers and a navy blazer. All in all we'd spent less than twenty pounds. I still didn't know where we were going but I didn't care. I was with Luke; we were laughing and window shopping in the middle of London. Everything was going to be okay.

"I'd love an apartment in New York city when I'm older," I said wistfully; "just off central park, somewhere in the middle of it all; imagine that."

"That'd be pretty cool alright. I'm thinking though that Dubai is the place to be. I mean look at how much money everyone who goes there makes."

"True," I said, "maybe we should just buy a beach house in California and be hippies; that sounds easy."

"Now, that is definitely something I'm down for. Man a secret part of me has always wanted a ponytail."

We both laughed, Luke looked at his watch that I had got him for his 17th birthday.

"God, almost 3; we better hurry," he said tugging me along faster. We were near London Bridge at this stage. We took a couple of turns and back alleyways and then we were on Thomas

Street. I started to guess where we were headed but that would be crazy so I didn't say it out loud.

"Here we are my lady," exclaimed Luke, stopping outside the shard building. I froze.

"You're not serious," I said slowly.

"Quick now, we're late for our reservation," he opened the door and we walked towards the lift. Luke pressed for the 31st floor.

"Our reservation?" I asked.

"Lunch is a lot cheaper than dinner," winked Luke. I couldn't believe it. I had been obsessed with coming up here to eat in the restaurant at the top of one of the tallest buildings in London with the most amazing view. I had never come because I guess you needed a good reason to come to an expensive restaurant like this and I never had one. I could not wait to see the view.

The elevator doors opened and there it was. All of London and beyond; stretching out further and further.

"I wanted to show you that it's a big world," whispered Luke; leading me out into the restaurant and bar.

"It is," I said back.

"Good afternoon," a lady dressed in a stylish waitress uniform came up to us.

"Reservation for Luke," said Luke confidently. Dressing up had certainly been a good idea I thought as I looked around. There must have been some sort of work function on because there were a few big groups of people all incredibly dressed up.

"Oh yes here you are, follow me Mr and Miss Fray; we got for you; as requested one of the best views in the house." She led us towards the front of the restaurant; directly in front of the massive windows. There was a table for two. We sat down and she left us to decide what to order; promising us a bottle of champagne was on its way.

"Mr and Miss Fray," I laughed once she had walked away.

"I know right, I booked with my dad's 'only for emergencies credit card' though and that's the name on it."

"Luke!" I exclaimed, "He's going to freak out! And the champagne too."

"He'll be fine; this is an emergency of sorts. Food is essential right? Especially when you're pregnant," he said in lower voice.

"Oh I can't actually drink, but your right I suppose we will have to order double right," I smiled.

"Triple," nodded Luke.

The waitress came back with the champagne and I asked for a non-alcoholic cocktail along with our orders. We went slightly overboard, ordering three starters and three mains.

"We're celebrating," said Luke, clinking his glass to mine.

"We are?" I asked taking a sip.

"Yes, under any other circumstances a guy and a girl in love would be over the moon to have a baby on the way right? So why shouldn't we?"

I could see his point. It was all a matter of how you viewed what was socially acceptable.

"Yeah you are right," I said, "but our whole futures Luke." He put up his hand.

"We still have them Amy, they just might be a little different now. You can still be a nurse and I can still study Law but we can do it in our own time. We can make it work for us. We'll be like one of those super modern new families, nothing happens the way it used to now anyways."

"Do you actually think we can do this?" I asked.

"Think? Amy I know we can. I could never imagine my life without you even before all of this happened so no way was I ever letting you go. Our life together is just going to have an earlier start than everyone else's right?"

"You know, when you put it like that, you make it sound pretty exciting," I smiled, tucking into our food that had just arrived.

"It is Amy; it will be."

"Now let's talk about names," I said, my whole mood picking up. *This could work*, I thought. We could do this, Luke and me. We were different from the rest; we wouldn't fall apart or become failures of parents. So we sat there, the whole of London by our side as the daylight got darker, we ordered dessert and then seconds and soon enough all of the stars were out and the moon was full. We had been here for hours. We stared out into the night sky.

"Look," I said, pointing out a shooting star that flew past.

"Make a wish," said Luke closing his eyes.

I closed mine too, and I wished. I wished for Luke and I to be good parents and I wished for everything to be okay; and in that moment, I actually believed it would.

Of course perfect moments can't last forever. And eventually the waitress did tell us another couple had arrived for their reservation. Luke paid for everything with his dad's 'emergency credit card' and we walked out into the night air, full and laughing.

"It's time to head home Amy," said Luke as we walked towards the tube.

"Oh dear, for a brief moment I forgot about that place," I laughed.

"Will your parents be okay?" he asked.

"They'll be fine," I lied, I knew they had probably been searching for me all day and were in the midst of a panic attack.

"Mine will get it I think," contemplated Luke, "I mean Mum will, she's like in love with you after the other day. Did I tell you that?"

"No," I laughed, "what did she say?"

"Oh she just thinks you're so mature and good for me."

I laughed, "I'm good for you?"

"Bizarre, I know." He rolled his eyes cheekily.

We arrived at my stop and I got up to get off.

"Love you," I said.

"Love you too, text me when your home," said Luke and the doors shut between us. My feet hurt as I walked home, these sandals were definitely a size too small. I was glad no one was out on our street to see me, earlier it had felt like we were in a different country not our home city. Thank god no one had seen us I smiled.

I reached my front door and before I could even knock it opened. Dad was there. "She's home," he bellowed before pulling me into a tight, tight hug.

I was expecting the usual shouts and roars from Dad and the typical tears and stern voice from Mum but no, after Dad hugged me he brought me into the kitchen where Mum and Mike were sitting.

"Oh my gosh, Amy, what happened?" cried Mum.

"Amy seriously, you need to stop shocking us all the time. I need my time to be the rebellious teenager okay, you're taking it all away from me," mocked Mike.

"I'm so sorry," I started looking at all of them, "I'll forgive you," joked Mike.

"Don't worry about it Amy, you don't need to apologise for anything, let me run to the bathroom and then we can all talk, just sit tight and relax," Dad ran up the stairs.

I raised my eyebrows and looked at Mum and Mike. *What a change of tune*, I thought. From a man who hadn't looked me in the eyes for two months to a man who suddenly wanted me to relax.

"You being gone really gave him a shock Amy," said Mum quietly.

"Yeah he finally copped on and was blaming himself, thought you might have done a runner or god knows what…" continued Luke.

"He thought it was his fault…because of all the harsh words he said," sighed Mum. "I know you knew he didn't mean them and I tried to tell him that but still…"

"I don't know," said Mike. "Honestly I think it was what he needed to realise there are far worse things than you being pregnant…"

I smiled at him. Dad returned.

"Amy, can I just say?"

I put up my hand.

"Dad, don't worry. I know what you're going to say and you don't need to."

"No, Amy, I was wrong I treated you awfully and then when you were gone all I could think about was how awful I've been, how cruel and how un-loving and how if god forbid anything happened to you, the last way I would have been was a terrible, terrible dad."

I looked at him and reached out my arms. He hugged me.

"I needed to acknowledge how lucky I was, sometimes we need to be scared a little to help us realise how lucky we are."

I nodded, he sat down beside me. I knew they were all wondering what had happened. So I filled them in from start to finish, all of the Luke and I dressing up, included.

"That's an awful dress though," commented Mike, looking me up and down. I whacked him across the table.

"So, ehm Amy, did you and Luke talk about your choices now then?" asked Mum worriedly.

I told them we'd decided to keep the baby, I left out the fact that we'd already decided on names and all of that; *one step at a time*, I thought.

Dad took a deep breath but before he could say anything Mum interrupted.

"You do understand what that will mean right?"

I nodded.

"Of course we will give you all the help you need but it won't be our baby, it'll be yours…" said Mum.

"It's an idea…" started Dad.

"Look, we have spent the whole day talking it over, Luke and I and he's going to talk to his parents too but what we think is we will both take a year out from college, I mean we will just defer any offers we get. We will work and hopefully everything will be okay right?" Saying it out loud I was aware how unrealistic the whole plan was. I mean were we going to live together? We couldn't afford even a tiny place in London and did we even want to live together? It had all seemed a lot more rose tinted in the candlelit restaurant.

"Okay," Mum said slowly, "look Amy, I understand that you and Luke love each other very much but have you really thought about this?"

I stalled, *no*, I thought, *no I hadn't but if I was going to be mature I may as well start pretending that I was.*

"Yes. I mean we know it will be difficult and I don't want to put anything on you…"

"Well…" started Dad, "there are other options right…"

Mum interrupted, she looked tired, "Look I suppose it's good that you two have decided what you want." She shot Dad a look. "So let's just take it slow from here and we will definitely figure it all out. Keeping the baby is possible, once we all work together; it mightn't be the image you see in your head Amy, you do understand that life isn't like that."

"Yeah," nodded Dad, "who knows, you mightn't have to defer college; we will figure it out."

I knew what he was implying, that I could go locally and Mum could take care of the baby. But it was my baby; I didn't want that. I kept my mouth shut though, it was late and I could sort it all out later. What I really wanted was a bath and bed.

"Okay," I said getting up to leave.

"Oh by the way Amy; Lily was calling for you. She sounded worried," said Luke, making a face. I made one back.

"Okay, I'll call her. I'm just going to have a bath and go to bed."

Twenty minutes later I was in the tub; I turned my phone back on. Dozens of message from both Tara and Lily; I had forgotten they would be expecting me in school. As I was looking through them my phone started buzzing, Lily. I slid across to answer.

"Hey," I said.

"Hey you, how is everything?" asked Lily anxiously.

"Oh good," I was trying to think of a valid excuse, "I just was really ehm, sick, like stomach and..."

"Oh I called earlier and Mike said you were visiting your aunt Cindy, that she was sick..."

I intervened quickly, stupid Mike, "Oh god yeah, she was sick and I was sick so ehm...I said I'd bring her over stuff cause you know, I can't get ehm sicker..."

"Right," said Lily slowly, "so are you okay then?"

"Yeah of course why wouldn't I be?" I asked, sounding sharper than I intended.

"Whoa, chill just wondering, like you are sick. What exactly is wrong then?" Her tone contained sarcasm and suspicion.

"It's ehm kind of awkward Lily, you don't want to know." I didn't know what I was saying but I needed her to believe me.

"Oh my god no. Have you got an STD?" cried Lily from the other end of the phone. *Great,* I thought. Look at the new mess I've gotten myself in.

"No, no," I said quickly but then I had an idea. "A UTI, I just need to pee all the time, it's awful. Sorry for being so shady." I lied, my face going red even though she wasn't there to see it.

"Oh shit Amy, I am sorry; I shouldn't have pushed you."

"You're alright," I said, laughing in an attempt to ease the situation. "I should be okay by tomorrow. I got some stuff from the doctor..."

"Fabulous because we are having a sleepover on Friday at mine! Me you, Tara and hell of a lot of food and champagne; I'm going to get all your favourites."

I didn't know what to say, usually I loved out girl's nights in with just us three, but it was getting harder and harder to spend time with them whilst keeping this massive secret. I felt like everything I said was a lie even if it wasn't.

"Oh Lily…" I tried to think of a valid excuse.

"No excuses," said Lily before I could. "I feel like I'm losing you and Tara and she agreed to come and she's the harder one," she laughed, "so were having a re-bonding night whether you like it or not."

I sighed. "Of course, I'll be there," I said, "and don't worry Lily, you're not losing us. I think we're all just a bit stressed probably."

"Yeah you're right, alright Amy, goodnight and I hope you sleep well and don't need to pee too much," she laughed before hanging up. I knew avoidance was not something I could do forever, especially after today, but right now; it was the only think I knew how to do.

Chapter 11

It was Friday night and the three of us were sitting on Lily's bed. Surrounded by untouched food and drink; luckily Lily hadn't really noticed yet.

"So, I've been thinking and I don't want to be a virgin going into college," said Lily out of nowhere.

"What?" I blurted out and reached for a handful of M&M's, my favourite.

"Well I just don't, I mean I don't want to just do it with anyone but I mean I want to get it done."

Tara was nodding. "I know what you mean, but I don't actually feel the need to have it done. Everyone thinks I have anyways," she shrugged. It was true, Tara was so confident and boys were always after her so everyone just presumed she had it done a long time ago. Even a part of me always thought maybe she just had and never told me. After Luke and I did it though I knew she hadn't, she would have told me then. If we could share anything we did.

"Yeah, so true but see everyone knows I'm innocent, so everyone just has this presumed idea of me. I mean I don't want people to know about me having sex but I want to, I don't know, I want to do it for myself. So I know."

"It's a big step thought Lily I mean are you sure?" I was just now hyper cautious of the aftermaths of it rather than the doing.

"Well just don't get pregnant," laughed Tara. I froze. "But you know what Lily, I think your right. After all it's your life, you take control and decide what you want to do eh, don't let the boys decide or society decide right?"

Tara, like us all, was a real feminist but she was the best at making us realise our worth and pushing the boundaries of what we deemed normal when really anything was normal and society just put us into boxes.

Lily nodded and sipped her drink. "I've decided to take things into my own hands," said Tara. I froze, was she about to talk about it…

Lily looked her intently too, she was dying to know what was going on I knew.

Tara looked at me. "I've decided to start acting again," she said simply. I hadn't realised I was holding my breath until she said this and I let it out. Why was I so worried about Tara telling her secret? Did I think it meant I was an even worse person for not telling mine? Was my secret only okay because I knew others were also keeping ones or did I just not want to feel so alone in keeping secrets; did I want to know there were others like me.

"Ah Tara that's so brilliant!" cried Lily, jumping up on the bed.

"I've been thinking about it for a while and I know I did want medicine but it's just not me at the moment and ever since I quit two years ago I've always wanted to go back!" said Tara, grinning from ear to ear.

"Aw Tara I'm so happy for you, this is brilliant. Are you going to go back to your old theatre group?" I asked.

"No, I actually got accepted to a really good one in west end. I went for an interview last weekend and they accepted me!" she squeaked out the last bit with excitement.

"Oh Tara this is so great! Time to celebrate! I made us cake earlier because you know why not!" said Lily. Tara's face dropped.

"Oh I'm so full," I started

"Okay, ooh Mum's got some bottles of champagne left over from her book club last night; shall I sneak them up?"

It was my faces turn to fall. This was going to be a tricky night, time for some more lies.

"Antibiotics," I said, pointing vaguely to my below area.

"Huh?" asked Tara.

Here we go again I thought and I launched into my UTI story, lies were very messy indeed.

Chapter 12
April

I was back in Dr Fosters; this time it was Luke sitting by my side and not my mum. That felt weird, but I guess weird was the most common emotion I felt these days. I was becoming super conscience that I was going to start showing.

"Seeing as you've such a small frame Amy, you don't appear to be showing at all, but don't worry everything is going fine and the baby is healthy! Now in a week or two we can do a scan to find out the baby's sex; if of course you want to?"

I looked at Luke. "I think we've had enough surprises," he said, smiling at me. Dr Foster smiled, she liked him. Everyone did; it was actually very annoying. I pushed the thought to things to think about later. Put it persisted, he was so eager about the baby and the amazing future it was going to have, our parents had started to admire his determination. I don't know why but his joy and eagerness was really starting to bug me.

"Yeah, Luke's right," I agreed, ignoring my negative thoughts. "I don't want anything extra to worry about or think about."

"Okay perfect, well then at the end of the month we will have the scan; until then just keep taking your vitamins, eating healthy and try and do some light exercise daily okay?"

I nodded. I was sick of hearing what I should be doing but I smiled because Dr Foster was kind and I was just tired.

"Yeah, we've been trying right Amy?" said Luke.

"Uh huh," I said, getting ready to leave.

"Is there any more we can, just to make sure the baby is as healthy as possible?" he asked.

"Luke, we're fine," I said, god why did he try so hard to be perfect at everything.

Dr Foster could see my patience was on the verge. "I think Amy's doing very well," she said.

"So there's nothing more we could be doing? Is there like classes or something?" asked Luke, I was ready to shout at him.

"Your baby is progressing perfectly," said Dr Foster calmly looking at me.

"See Luke," I snapped. "We'll have a perfect baby; just like you. Now let's go," I opened the door and walked out.

"Sorry about that," I heard Luke say to Dr Foster which obviously only made me madder. "She's coping with a lot, I need to be better," he continued, which of course was such a kind thing to say but at this moment in time it only pissed me off even more. I walked out into the street.

"Amy, wait up," shouted Luke after me outside.

I spun around. "You don't need to apologise for me you know? I don't need you to look after me, I'm fine. The baby's fine so quit it," I said continuing to walk.

"Amy what's going on? Do you feel sick? Should we go back to the doctors?" He put his hand on my forehead. "Your hot and you don't look good, are you sure you don't feel sick?"

I lost it. "I don't feel sick Luke I'm pregnant, and I don't look good because I…" I started speaking slowly, "I am pregnant, I'm fucking pregnant!!!" I burst into tears and Luke tried to wrap his arm around me.

"Just leave me alone," I said and I walked away, I didn't look back.

The First Time Luke and I Fought

"But you could do amazing things Amy?" Luke had said about six months earlier when we were filling out our UCAS applications at his house.

"What do you mean?" I asked, genuinely not knowing.

"Well you know, you're a really smart girl, there'll be a lot of not smart people on your course," he said awkwardly.

"Luke, just because it doesn't require many points doesn't mean it isn't hard, being a nurse isn't easy," I said blandly. What we wanted to do in the future had never posed a major topic in our conversations, now at this time in our lives; it was almost all we spoke about.

"Yeah, yeah I get that; but do you not want to do more than say change an old person's diaper or take some little kids blood?" he asked.

I looked up at him. "Did you seriously just say that? Honestly Luke it's so much more than that," I said, sounding angry with him for the first time ever.

"Look don't get angry, it's only because I want what's best for you, you know that right? And I just believe in you so much that I know you're going to make such a difference in this world. I don't want you to settle," he said softly.

I knew where he was coming from, and in a way he was right. I was smart but often tests didn't suit me or I didn't suit them; whichever it was they weren't a reflection of me. Luke knew I was anxious about never achieving enough, so I didn't really push myself too he was right. But I wanted to be a nurse.

"I want to help people Luke, in a small way. I don't need my name to be known half way around the world. I can make an impact in a smile, or a conversation or just a hand to hold." My voice was getting louder, "and if that isn't good enough for you then that's your problem."

"Whoa Amy, chill," he said, his voice harsher than ever, "I just think you can be better, do better I don't know, leave the nursing jobs to people who can't actually do anything else."

I stood up, gathering my forms. "I'm going," I said briskly, "call me when you've grown up if you ever do." I walked out the door.

"Jesus Christ Amy!" Luke shouted after me, "You don't need to be such a moody bitch."

I slammed the door behind me.

That night Luke called me,

"I needed to grow up; I'm really sorry."

I stayed silent on the other end of the line.

"You're going to be amazing in whatever you do; and your right, a nurse is so much more than what I said. Very few can make a good one but I know you will. I'm so sorry; I love you."

"Will you help me write my personal statement tomorrow then?" I asked cheekily.

"There's nothing I'd love more," he said.

"Okay," I said, smiling.

"Get your sleep, I'll see you tomorrow."

"Love you," I said.
"I love you too and Amy?" said Luke
"Yeah."
"Let's never fight again, not even a little okay."
"Okay," I said.
"You promise?" he asked,
"Promise," I said before hanging up.
And we never did break our promise.

I arrived home in a terrible mood, and when I walked in it didn't help that Mum and Dad were literally hopping in the kitchen, they wanted to know every update on the baby and every last detail of the appointment. I wouldn't call it excitement; I think they just wanted to feel more in control but where had all this eagerness come from I thought as they fired questions at me. When did baby go from being the absolute end of the world to something they were now actually concerned about? And more importantly why did I feel so weird about the whole damn thing.

"It was fine," I said, "no news."

"Oh but there must be news; how was Dr Foster and how did Luke get on, he didn't freak out did he?" asked Mum.

"And is it healthy and good and are you healthy? Do we need to get more iron in your diet? Or is that right, I forget?" said Dad, looking confused.

"Everything's fine I said, we don't need any more iron or whatever the hell it is," I snapped, sitting down at the table and resting my hands in my head. I was just so tired. I wished everyone could shut up about the stupid baby.

"Amy, that's no way to speak to us; what's going on, is everything alright?" asked Dad sitting down opposite me.

"I am fine," I said, "I just want to stop talking about the baby okay."

"Well Amy; it is happening. This is the way your life is going to be now. You made this choice remember," said Mum, no sympathy in her voice.

"I know that mum but…"

"No buts Amy, this is it. We're trying our hardest to do what's right and all you're doing is giving us lip," said Dad sternly. So as you can guess, for the second time that day I lost it and I shouted them.

"All you care about now is the stupid baby that isn't even real yet, it's not that exciting okay? It's just a thing that's happening, it doesn't need to take over our lives right? I'm going to my room." I walked away before they could intervene and I just fell into my bed. It was six p.m. and I slept until eight the next morning. Maybe I was just really tired right? Things would be better at school.

Luke walked straight past me in the hallway. Not even glancing my way.

"What was that?" asked Tara outright once he was past us. I shrugged my shoulders. Speaking meant more lying and I just didn't have the imagination anymore. Pretending to need to pee so often had really drained me that week.

"Amy, what's going on?' asked Lily, looking concerned. "Do you need us to talk to him?"

"What?" I snapped, "I don't need you to do anything."

They both looked shocked, I never raised my voice.

"Sorry, I'm so sorry I'm just tried and Luke, he's just stressed over exams; we'll be fine once they ease off."

"Don't worry about it Amy, everyone's at their breaking points."

"Well," smiled Lily, "I've got something that will take all your minds off boy drama and stress!"

Both Tara and I rolled our eyes, here we go again. Another one of Lily's infamous plans.

"So this Saturday; Mum and Dad are gone away so you know what that means!" she said.

"A party?" asked Tara, excitedly. Tara loved a party; like she never ever missed one. One time she broke her leg the day before and she still made it to Luke's 16th.

"Yes, of course and let's make it a big one, Friday night so we have all day Saturday to clean up," Lily was super excited. "What you think Amy? Are you in?"

I had planned on going looking for Crystal this weekend, she wasn't retuning any of my calls and she hadn't been at our group in weeks, Deborah had no idea where she was. But I could hardly say that to the girls and not going was going to be harder to explain than going.

"Of course," I smiled, "that's exactly what we need; a good party."

"Great, well I'll make an event tonight, invite everyone," said Lily just as the bell rang and we all went our separate ways. Luke didn't sit beside me like he normally did in geography. I tried to not let it get to me; I was after all still mad at him wasn't I?

The next few days went by so slow. Not talking to Luke was a lot harder than anticipated and being at home was treacherous, everyone was on the verge of snapping so no one spoke. Mum and Dad's weird rush of excitement or anticipation over the baby had left just as quickly as it came. I didn't know if this was good or bad. Bizarrely, I was looking forward to Lily's; at least it would be a few hours of distraction.

I was sitting down with the girls for lunch on Friday when Luke came over to me. He didn't look happy, or apologetic; not that I expected either. I had been the bitch.

"Can you talk?" he asked roughly.

"Hi Luke," said Tara chirpily, good old Tara.

"Hey," he said barely looking at her or Lily, his eyes fixated on mine.

I nodded and got up. Lily squeezed my hand quickly as I walked by her. Luke brought me to outside his locker.

"Amy, what the hell was the other day about? I've been literally too angry to talk to you but we have," he lowered his voice, "a baby coming; we need to be mature."

I thought for a moment. "Do we?" I asked, "I mean we are only seventeen, why do we have to be mature?" My voice was getting louder, "why do we have to be happy and mature and excited huh? Who says what the right way to act is? I want to be young and stupid; I don't want to be mature." I crossed my arms over my chest defiantly. Luke looked at me like he didn't know who I was.

He whispered aggressively, "Amy, you're pregnant! And I love you to bits and I want to make this work but you're losing it."

I took a step back. "I'm losing it? I asked, laughing, "I'm not the one who wants to pick out outfits or names, I mean what? Have you forgotten that this isn't the best thing in the world? Have you forgotten you had a life to live, dreams to fulfil?"

"No Amy, stop it." Luke almost shouted and a few people heard us. Luke looked around.

"Just stop it, I'm trying my best," he said softly. "I'll see you later," he said and he walked away. People whispered around us. I walked quickly past them and back to Lily and Tara.

They looked at me anxiously.

"We'll be okay," I said, smiling weakly, "small drama. Let's not dwell on it, what's the plan for tonight then?" I asked.

Lily, ever the party planner, was happy to launch into the details of how many she was expecting (over a hundred had clicked going) and how she had pre ordered pizza and told everyone to bring their own drink.

"Run home and get clothes after school and then come to mine afterwards, we can set up and have ourselves a little pre party."

Tara made a whoop sound. "It's not dressy is it?" I asked, thinking of what I'd look like in a tight black dress.

"Wear your lace black dress that always looks good," said Tara, *mind reader,* I thought.

"It tore," I lied quickly but continued talking so I didn't have to think up how. "I might just wear jeans tonight. I'm feeling I'm going to want to eat a lot of pizza."

Lily laughed, "go for it, you always look good casual anyways, and don't worry there will be plenty of pizza."

The bell rang for last class.

"See you all at mine," Lily said and we all walked off.

Chapter 13

"Lily's drunk," whispered Tara furiously to me as I walked into Lily's house. I was a bit later than I'd said I'd be but it was only eight o'clock.

"What?" I mouthed to Tara, there was only a few of our closer group milling around in the kitchen.

Tara was about to speak when there was a loud high pitched squeal from upstairs.

"AMMMMYYYYYYY..." cried Lily, stumbling down, "MY best BEST friend; oh my god don't worry Tara," she wrapper her arms floppingly around the two of us. "You are BOTH my bestest friends in the entire world," she was stuttering, "even... Even if YOU LIE hahahahaha," she laughed hysterically and pulled us out to arm's length. I exchanged a look with Tara.

"Oh my god I'm kidding, I love you guys like so, so, so a lot and much and let me get you a drink and," she started jumping up and down happily.

Tara looked so angry, I grabbed Lily's arm, "shall we go upstairs and I'll get you some water Lil," I said; trying to stay calm.

"Why don't you trust me?" she asked suddenly, her mood changing.

"Ehm, what?" I said slowly, looking to Tara.

"Lily, you don't know what you're talking about. You're drunk and people are about to arrive okay."

Lily laughed. "Guys I'm joking, I love you so much let's go upstairs and I'll tell you all about my 'hehe' PLAN," she pulled us upstairs after her. From the corner of my eye I spotted Luke talking to Sam in the kitchen. I didn't think they'd be here already, we made eye contact and he looked as though he was about to leave Sam and walk towards me, but Lily yanked my hand and they were out of sight.

Lily and Her Drink and Why I'm Probably a Terrible Person

When Lily and I first became friends she didn't drink. We were only fifteen but by the time we were sixteen she had called me and Tara on numerous occasions, drunk and alone. It was so out of her character and no one but us knew about it which is why her getting publicly drunk at a party was so bizarre to us. Neither of us understood Lily's drinking; until one night.

My phone rang; I was over at Luke's on a Saturday night, we were nearing the end of our second last year in school.

"Who is it?" he asked, we were watching a movie.

"Just Lily," I said, I ignored it and sent her a text saying I would call her later but my phone kept buzzing.

"I'd better take this," I said to Luke, who nodded as I stepped out into the hall.

"Lily," I said once she picked up.

"Is, is that YOU?" she asked before bursting into tears.

"Lily what's going on? We need to –" I knew she was drunk immediately, this was getting tiring but she was my best friend. I needed to help her.

"I need you," she whispered quietly.

"I'm coming," I said and hung up. I was ready to get to the bottom of what was going on with Lily.

I left Luke in a hurry, telling him there was girl drama. I rode his bike over to Lily's. She was one of those lucky few Londoners who lived in a mansion of a house. I parked my bike around the back and let myself in.

Lily was sitting at the kitchen table, nursing a glass of red wine. I sat down beside her.

"I need to stop," she said, she was still drunk but her words were perfect.

"What's going on Lily?" I asked.

"It's Kirsten," she said slowly, Kirsten was Lily's older sister; she'd left for university in Aberdeen.

"Is she alright?" I asked.

"She, she was in an accident," said Lily.

I was confused; Lily had started drinking like this about four months ago; how was this connected?

"She took drugs, at a party one night and she was missing for two days." Lily took a deep breath, "when the police found her she was all battered and bruised and her clothes...they were all torn."

"Oh my god Lily, that's terrible. Why didn't she come home? Is she alright now?" I asked.

"They took her to hospital, Mum and Dad went over... they wouldn't let me go," a tear rolled down her face, "they were so ashamed Amy. They blamed her because she took the drugs they thought it was all her fault. It wasn't."

I nodded, "of course it wasn't."

"She's in a private hospital over there now, what happened to her caused some major mental health issues I think. They barely visit her and they lie to everyone about where she is, they hate to admit that their perfect girl isn't so perfect anymore. I don't want to be perfect Amy; if that's the price I pay," Lily's voice rose and she threw her empty wine glass at the wall.

I stood up and walked over to her and pulled her up into my arms. I didn't know what to do.

"So that's why," I said, referring to her drinking.

"That's why. I wanted them to think I wasn't so perfect either, so maybe they'd start to love Kirsten again..." She paused for breath, "but they don't even notice Amy. They're never home much anymore. They don't even notice," she shouted.

"It's okay," I said softly, "you've got me and Tara; we will help you. You don't need to do this anymore; there are other ways."

"I know," she said, looking down, "do you want to stay the night?"

"Sure," I said, smiling.

A few hours later, Lily was sobered up and we were sitting watching movies and eating food. She'd told me all about Kirsten's situation and it was awful how terribly it had affected her.

We went to bed nattering away and she promised to never drink like that again.

I was just about to fall asleep when she whispered my name

"Amy," I let out a noise but I don't think she heard me.

"There's another thing," she whispered so softly I could barely hear her, *"I've always been kind of in love with Luke."*

I froze under my duvets. She couldn't still be drunk I thought to myself.

"I'm sorry," she continued quietly, *"but before you even moved here I was. I tried to tell you; in the early days but you got closer to him quicker than you got closer to me…"*

I stayed perfectly still. This couldn't be happening, she was my best friend and she was going through an awful time. I should say something shouldn't I? But what could I say, I loved Luke and despite knowing that my friends were more important I still loved him too much.

"It's okay though, I think I'm over it. I mean I see you two together all the time. I'm so over it' she turned over in her bed. *"I think,"* she said.

I pretend to be asleep.

The next morning when we were eating breakfast Lily said she was sorry for any drunken thoughts she had late last night.

"Don't worry, I fell asleep pretty quick," I lied.

"I'm going to stop drinking I swear and please don't say anything to anyone about Kirsten, I'll tell Tara but no one else."

I nodded, "Of course."

"Thanks Amy," she said smiling.

And she never did drink like that again; only occasionally on a night out and never alone. We never spoke about the times she did and we rarely mentioned Kirsten. In every relationship there are a lot of unwritten rules and unspoken of secrets. People are more complicated than you'd ever guess.

Luke was never mentioned like that again either, and in my mind I pretended it never happened because if I acknowledged that perhaps I had ignored warning signs of her fondness for Luke then wasn't I a part of the reason she started to drink. If I admitted I heard her, wasn't I a terrible friend to the girl who showed me kindness when barely anyone did?

"Two words," said Lily; swaying around the upstairs bathroom; both Tara and I were sitting in the tub. We hadn't seen or heard her this drunk in ages.

"Go on," said Tara impatiently.

"Joshua Jules," said Lily and slugged back the glass of water we had given her.

"Cute Joshua?" I asked, "In the year below us?"

Lily nodded eagerly.

"Oh no," said Tara, "not for?"

Lily nodded, even more eager than before. I; however was still confused.

"What?" I asked.

"S E X," spelled out Lily and laughed but I could see she wasn't as drunk as she had been before. "I need more vodka," she said quickly, the same fact dawning on her.

"Oh," I said.

"Well he is cute, but he is also young," pointed out Tara, getting into the plan now.

"Yes true but that's good I think," said Lily, suddenly sober, "it means he's most likely a VIRGIN yayyyy," she yelled the last bit. I couldn't help but laugh.

"Shhh," said Tara giggling.

"You want a virgin?" I asked.

"Yes, that way," she paused for effect, "we both will be awful!"

The three of us burst out laughing as Lily did a little dance. I guess she deserved to have a fun night and do whatever it was she wanted. *She'd been working hard and she was feeling isolated*, I thought.

"You go for it, tonight?" asked Tara.

"TONIGHT IS GONNA BE A NIGHT… TO REMEMBER," sang Lily at the top of her lungs. Suddenly there was a knock on the bathroom door.

"Amy," said a boy's voice from outside. I hopped out of the tub, Tara did too.

"Luke," I said, unlocking the door.

"Hey, can we talk?" he took in Lily and Tara, "hey guys."

"Sure, ehm…"

"Let's go greet our guests," cried Lily grabbing Tara and pulling her with her.

"Come on in, welcome to my home." I joked once they'd left, beckoning Luke into the bathroom. It was time to set things straight. Luke was right, I was being childish.

"I'm sorry," I started but Luke's face told me I should go no further.

"You're sorry," he laughed, "hah, Amy I think it's a little bit late for that." He took a step closer and I could smell the beer on his breath.

"Have you been drinking?" I asked surprised. Luke never drank like, never; it actually pissed me off because I knew he just did it to make everyone think he was better than needing alcohol to have a good time. It was another box to tick in his list of having perfect traits. I sounded like a bitch in my head, didn't I?

"Yeah; I actually have Amy, have you got a problem with that or is it not good enough for you?"

"What are you talking about Luke, of course I don't care if you drink; why would you say that?" I was pissed off he thought that he had to be good for me.

"Oh you know right well, you are always looking down on people from your high and mighty chair of being the nice girl hah! You're so nice it hurts Amy, be a bitch for once in your life and don't apologise for it."

"Luke, what the hell, what are you talking about?" I asked angrily.

"I'm never going to be good enough for you and I try so hard ahh," he cried out. I tried to grab his arm, "Please Amy, don't. I don't want to do this now, you're right, I'm drunk and I'm saying stupid stuff."

"Just stop," I said quickly, "we don't need to fight anymore."

Luke opened the bathroom door, "Yes Amy, we do."

He walked out and I followed him, it felt like a reversal of the doctor's appointment.

"Luke! Come back," I yelled down the hall.

"I'm sorry Amy I fucking love you so much but no," and with that he turned around and kept walking. I leaned against the doorframe and started to cry. Tara appeared at the top of the stairs and came over to me.

"What's going on sweetie you can tell me," she said leading me back into the bathroom. I couldn't tell her, but I could cry. So I did.

Chapter 14

While I was gathering myself together in the bathroom; Luke was having his loyalties truly tested downstairs.

"Hey Luke pass me the mixers will you?" called Lily from across the kitchen counter. Luke, with his head and heart still pounding passed her the coke and Fanta silently. Lily's fingers purposely lingered on Luke's.

"My god Luke, your hands are so cold; are you alright?"

Her pretty voice rang octaves above the loud house music and peoples mindless chatter. Luke looked up at her. She really had gotten pretty in the last few months, he thought, taking in her V-necked red dress, she'd grown into herself. Luke looked down quickly as he realised he was staring. He's never looked at her like that before; *god*, he thought, it had been years since he'd looked at anyone but Amy in that way.

Lily saw his mind falter and she grabbed the opportunity.

"Come with me," she mouthed, her smile lay and cheeky. She was sick of being nothing but a good friend yet always being left in the dark, she knew both Amy and Tara were hiding things from her.

She beckoned with her finger for Luke to follow her, and he did.

Out in the back garden; the cold night air shook Luke and for a second he stopped walking and thought of Amy.

"Coming?" asked Lily sweetly; turning around to face him. Her pretty features were even more accentuated in the dark and her long hair had fallen naturally down by her side.

Luke was torn but he was also tired of being a good person, a good son, a good boyfriend. None if it was helping the situation. He followed Lily to the bench swing at the end of the garden. He sat down next to her and she passed him the spare drink in her hand. The swing swayed a little under their weight and the movement made him feel dizzy; he really had never drunk before.

"I think I might get sick," Luke said suddenly.

Lily bolted up right as he leaned over his legs. She started to rub his back.

"Shhh, you'll be okay."

"I'm fine," he said, remembering himself and shaking her off gently.

"Is everything okay Luke? You seem stressed."

Luke didn't say anything, one word, one slip he thought and everything could come crashing down. And he didn't trust himself not to say something in the state he was in.

"You know you can tell me? I'm not just Amy's friend; I knew you before her."

Luke looked up at her; she brushed her hair slowly with her fingers, gazing back at him.

"Things are…" Luke started.

"Complicated?" offered Lily, "trust me, I know. We're so young it's crazy, you're such a good boyfriend, I mean like it must be hard…" She drawled out her last few words, moving closer to Luke.

Luke either didn't notice, or was too scared to acknowledge that he did.

"Yeah," he continued, "it's not that, I don't know it's just a stressful and I just try so hard," he rested his hands in his hand.

"You don't need to, not with me," said Lily, her words and images blurring together as she wrapped her arms around Luke. He turned to face her and they locked eyes, their faces mere inches apart.

I left the bathroom and walked down the stairs with Tara.

"You will be fine, he loves you to bits Amy," is what Tara was saying when I walked out into the back garden and saw two figures in what looked like to be seconds from a kiss.

"Luke," I called out weakly, hoping fiercely that that wasn't his grey hoodie I thought I could make out.

Tara stalled briefly beside me before charging forward. I followed and after two more steps I could see them clearly.

"Lily?" said Tara, "what the fuck? Luke?"

I stopped walking and turned around.

"Amy, wait it's not," cried out Luke and I started to run back through the house; the party was in full swing now and I pushed past through all my classmates. I felt like my chest was on fire; I'd never felt this alive, this much pain before.

I ran out her front door and Luke caught me by my shirt. I spun around on the pavement.

"What?" I snapped.

"Amy, stop, listen!" he panted.

I turned around and kept walking.

"Amy," cried a girl's voice, Lily.

"Lily, leave her," shouted Tara after her, I stopped and turned around. Tara was holding Lily in the front garden. Luke was right behind me in the middle of the street. The moon was full and I could see his face fully.

"It wasn't what it looked like," he said quickly, "I was sick, I drank too much…"

"Amy I swear I would never," cried Lily.

"Go back inside," said Tara to her, ushering her inside and then joining Luke on the street.

"I don't care Luke," I shouted, "that's Lily, even though it shouldn't matter who it was and I." I stopped because Tara was there but I was almost too angry to care.

"I get that you're… Overwhelmed but no excuses… none." I turned to keep walking.

"Please Amy," he pleaded but I kept walking. Tara ran by my side.

"I'll come home with you," she said shrugging, "I'm tired anyways."

Despite it all I smiled and she wrapped her arm around my back.

I barely slept a wink all night; Tara was snoring next to me. I had a gazillion messages and missed calls from both Luke and Lily. I genuinely didn't even know what to think; I had never even thought about the possibility of Luke cheating. Especially not with someone like Lily, maybe I shouldn't have ignored what she had said to me a year ago. Maybe I should have looked further than my own life and realised that other people felt things too.

"Ugh so early," moaned Tara from beside me.

"I know, I'm sorry."

"Did you sleep at all?" she asked sitting up.

"Nope," I laughed.

"Okay great that means you're going to be hungry because we're going for breakfast," she hopped out of bed quicker than I'd ever seen her move at eight a.m. in the morning.

"Oh, do we have to? I really felt like not dressing today…" I said weakly flopping back onto my bed.

"Nope," Tara ripped the duvet off me, "what Lily did and Luke or whatever happened is terrible but we can't mope around in self-pity, we're going to fix it."

"So cold," I cried jumping up from my duvet-less bed and pulling on a hoodie.

"What do you mean fix it? We can't fix it?" I said.

"Maybe it's not what it seems," offered Tara, passing me a pair of jeans which I reluctantly pulled on, carefully hiding my tiny bump under the hoodie.

"I doubt that, that's what they always say," I said.

"Come on, let's go. We're meeting Lily," said Tara, looking down at her phone.

"Tara? What the hell no, I don't want to talk to her." I sat down.

"I know you don't but we need to find out the full story. Think about it Amy, you know Lily; remember how kind she is, she would never have done this… I know I sound harsh and on her side but you'll thank me in the long run. You love Lily."

I had to agree with her, I did love Lily; despite what I had seen the night before my mind was still racing to think of how I must have gotten the situation wrong. I willed there to be some sort of valid excuse.

"Okay," I said quietly, "but…" I thought of what she had whispered to me a year ago.

"No buts, let's go get pancakes," she grabbed my arm and lifted me up; "and Amy…I'm really, really sad this happened for you; I hope it's not the end of so many things you love."

My eyes prickled with tears. "Me too."

"Whatever happens, you've got me," she said just as the doorbell rang.

It was Luke; I almost shut the door in his face but Tara stopped me.

"Go in here," she said, pushing the two of us into my front living room and closing the door. I looked Luke up and down, he was wearing the same clothes as last night and he looked a wreck. His eyes were red and his hair was a mess.

"So," I said.

"Amy, I am so, so sorry and I know that is nowhere near enough."

"Luke, did you kiss my best friend?" I asked bluntly.

"NO! God no, Lily and I never kissed or anything no Amy I would never."

"Did you only not kiss her because I walked outside before you could?" This was my real question because I knew I hadn't seen them actually kiss but nothing else validates those sort of close head encounters right?

Luke faltered before finally looking me straight in the eye. "No, Amy. I would never; I had a moment. I'm sorry but I did. I had a moment where like you said… I wanted to be young and reckless. Just for a moment I wanted to forget about rules and boundaries and what I should do. I had a moment where I forgot what was most important to me. Amy I'm so sorry. You're what's most important to me."

Maybe I'm weak, and maybe I'm a fool. But I believed him and I won't apologise for being forgiving. I let him hug me and I hugged him back.

"We're okay?" he asked.

"We're okay," I agreed.

"Better than perfect?" he asked.

"Of course, now I have to go meet Lily…" was her name about to become awkward between us.

"Okay great, let's not make things weird with that. It was nothing; she's your best friend you're my girlfriend. We're friends yeah?" said Luke.

"Yeah, I agree."

Tara was making herself a cup of tea in the kitchen when I found her after saying goodbye to Luke.

"Well?" she asked anxiously.

I smiled and she let out a breath. "Oh thank god, that's one less thing to worry about. Now come on, Lily's waiting for us."

We raced out the door and got a bus into Victoria where we met Lily in our favourite quirky pancake parlour. She had

86

already ordered our favourites and they were just being brought out when we arrived.

She smiled weakly at me and got up to give me a hug. I didn't even have the energy to question her too much on it. I knew what I needed to know and I had to believe that these people loved me and were loyal. If I started doubting them now then where would I stop? Really I just wanted things to be okay so badly that I made them okay.

"I don't know why I drank again, I'm so sorry I promise to never again," Lily said.

"Look Lil, it was a rough night but everything's going to be okay. Just don't drink again and if you want to when your alone you know to call us right?"

Tara nodded in agreement and our conversations lead into the more light-hearted matter of when Lily really could have sex with Joshua, it was so great to feel natural around them again. In a way Lily and Luke almost doing something bad made me feel like less of a liar. We all laughed and drank coffee and ate. Even Tara.

Chapter 15
May

It's going to be a girl. When I told Mum she said it was time we had a serious talk. Just me and her this time; so that evening when Mike was at a friend's and Dad was still at work, we sat down at the kitchen table. I knew this had been coming.

"Amy, it's time. We need to talk about what you're really going to do," she said matter of factly.

"I've been pretty naïve haven't I?" I said thinking of what all the girls were saying at our sessions made me realise being a mother was not an easy job. I had known that obviously but for some reason I had fooled myself into thinking I was different; that I could do this.

"It's okay," said Mum, "you're young. But you do need to think about what your next step is."

"Mum, I know this is awful but…" my voice quivered, "but sometimes I regret not getting the abortion. If I had only not been so weak…" I looked down at my hands to avoid her eyes.

"Amy don't! Look you did what you had to do. There's no point in over-thinking it," she was being so straight, so un-sensitive. I wanted to be five again and have her feel more sympathy over my scratched knee.

"Okay," I said, "so what do I do?"

Mum looked at me and took a sip, "unfortunately that's up to you, but do you want to know what I think?"

She was probably going to tell me anyways so I told her to go ahead.

"I think you should go to college, I think Luke should too. I don't think you should give the baby up for adoption but I think it should stay here with me…"

"No, Mum," I interrupted but she held up her hand.

"You can't raise a child Amy and even if you tried, you'd be living here and it would be like I was raising it anyways. You need to understand that a child is a life; it isn't just going to be okay after spending a year with you. What will you do when you actually do go to college?"

I shrugged. I hadn't let myself think that far.

"Exactly, or your other choice is to give it up. But think about the regret that could come with that? Could you live every day knowing your child was out there without you?"

I thought about it. I'd thought about this before, adoption seemed like a good choice in my eyes. I was giving somebody a life wasn't I? But Mum was right, I would always wonder.

"I suppose you'd think about her a lot," I said.

Mum nodded, her face softened; "of course you would, and darling none of these choices are easy but just think; if the baby is here with me you can see her as much as you like and we can figure out with time how we decide who she is in our family; but at least she will be with her real family and you'll get to live out your life too."

When she put it all like that, it did sound like the best idea. But then I thought of Luke and I and how sure he was we could do it.

"I really, I just don't know," I said feebly. Mum pursed her lips.

"Well, you'll figure it out. I think we both know what's best," and with that she got up and went upstairs. I was more confused than ever.

In school everyone was too wrapped up in exams and study to notice anything about my slightly expanding stomach. I bought a bigger jumper and complained about stress eating; only ever when Tara wasn't there though.

"Oh I know what you mean," said Lily, one lunch when it was just me and her, "Tara hasn't gained any though…" Her voice trailed off, she must have been suspicious.

"She has a small build anyways," I said nonchalantly

"You don't think she needs our help do you?" asked Lily looking concerned, "I mean I've realised I'm pretty shit when it comes to actually acting on the things I see," she lowered her voice. "Like Amy, I know you've something on your mind these past few months. You always changing the subject and drifting off."

I tried to say something but Lily continued.

"Don't worry. You don't have to tell me. I get that, trust me. But just know that I'm always here and if I can help in any way; you don't even have to tell me why; but just I'm here okay," she smiled and passed me half her cookie.

"Thanks Lil," I said. Sometimes I wished I was as good a person as her. Maybe that's why she had so many friends growing up and I had none. It wasn't that big a mystery.

I was contemplating this when Sam walked over to us.

"Hey guys," he said shyly, Sam was always quiet. Maybe that's why he liked Tara, she was the opposite; in a good way obviously.

"Hey Sam, what's up?" asked Lily, offering him some of her cookie also.

He took a bit, "ehm I'm just looking for Tara."

"Oh she should be around here somewhere," I said, looking around, "here let me text her," I said, whipping out my phone I sent here a quick 'where u' message.

Just as it sent Tara walked around the corner, smiling.

"Hey, we were looking for you," said Lily as she walked over.

"Guess what!" said Tara excitedly, barely taking in the nervous looking Sam, shifting from side to side on his feet.

"What?" I asked.

"So, my theatre just called me. I went to the bathroom to answer them and they without me knowing! Put my name forward for a place in the London school of acting for next year! I made the shortlist!" she squealed excitedly.

"Oh my god Tara!" Lily jumped up and gave her a hug.

"Tara that's amazing I'm so proud," I said joining them.

"I can't believe it, I really thought I wasn't good enough…oh hey Sam," she said suddenly noticing him.

"Hey, sorry ehm oh god yeah well done that's so cool I didn't know you acted," he said nervously.

"Oh ya know, just a little side hobby to keep me busy," joked Tara flicking her hair for effect.

"You must be pretty good eh," said Sam.

Tara shrugged, "Hopefully anyways," she laughed, "anyways, what's going on with you?"

Lily and I exchanged a look.

"I actually, erm, wanted to talk to you…" He looked at the two of us, "alone… if that's okay."

Tara's usually confident and tall posture shrank down.

"Let's go get ready for class," said Lily.

"We'll leave you two to it," I said, giving Tara a thumbs up as I left. It baffled me that someone as shy and quiet as Sam made her nervous when she was able to flirt with the older and hotter boys in our area without even blinking.

"They would be adorable," said Lily as we walked away.

"Oh I know, I don't know why she gets so nervous," I said.

We were at our lockers packing our bags when Tara ran by.

"Hey Tara," I shouted after her.

"What happened?" asked Lily as she turned around. Tara looked pale.

"Uh, I feel so sick guys I've got to go home…" She turned and kept walking towards the office and out of our sight.

The bell rang. I looked at Lily,

"Should we go after her?" she asked.

"Let's leave her, maybe she needs some space," I said; thinking that an interrogation was the last thing Tara probably wanted right now. Whatever it was; she would eventually tell me.

"Okay," said Lily, "I'll catch up with you later."

I walked slowly to geography, meeting Luke outside.

I cowardly sent him a note in class, telling him briefly about my conversation with Mum.

'After school! X' he wrote back quickly and when the bell rang we hung back until we were the only two in the class.

"What do you mean Amy?" he asked.

"I don't know if we can do it Luke, I mean realistically."

"But…" he stopped, "yeah my parents are saying the same thing. I was just so, so confident we should, I mean what does that mean for us though?"

"It doesn't mean anything," I said, "we're still us, I don't know. We have time to think, let's get through these exams okay."

"Yeah, let's and…" he couldn't say anymore because Lily appeared at the door.

"Amy, Luke, I was just talking to Sam," she said quickly.

"Oh yeah, he wanted to talk to Tara earlier," said Luke, "did he get her?"

Lily walked in, "Yes and he wanted to ask her to be his date to his sister's wedding…"

"Ah that's great," I said.

"No but, she freaked out," said Lily throwing up her hands.

"What do you mean?" asked Luke, "Freaked out?"

"She like started rambling and then ran away, Sam was so embarrassed he thought that she just didn't want to turn him down straight. I told him there must be something going on, right Amy?"

I shook my head, "Yeah, there must be. Come on, let's go to hers. Luke call me later about that homework okay."

"Sure," he gave me a wink, "and I'll talk to Sam and see if I can get any more."

"Thanks Luke," said Lily and they looked at each other.

I knew there was nothing between but my stomach still flipped and I felt hot.

"Come on Lily," I said quickly, it came out harsher than intended. Things weren't at all bad between us because of that, in fact it had made us closer, that fact that we got over it together. But still, I do have limits.

We left the school and made our way to Tara's. She opened the front door to us.

"I knew it was you two," she said, letting us in.

"Are you okay?" asked Lily as we sat down in the living room.

"Look, I don't know how to explain this…"

"It's okay," I said, she looked all pent up and anxious. "Just take a deep breath."

"I think I need to go to the bathroom," she said, quickly hopping up. Lily and I waited.

"God I hope there's nothing really wrong, what if she is sick? What if she has like, some illness?" Lily wrung her hands, "I'm going to check on her," she said getting up.

I looked at the photographs on Tara's mantelpiece; there I was, smiling beside her when we both got matching fringes.

There she was showing off her newly pierced ears; you could see the back of my head behind hers, we were so young. We'd done so much together.

"Amy," said Lily, appearing at the doorway.

"Uh huh?" I said standing up.

She beckoned me towards her with her finger and I followed her to outside the bathroom.

"Listen," she mouthed.

Inside the door I got hear Tara retching. *Shit*, I thought. It was happening again. I pushed on the door handle. It wasn't locked. Tara was standing up by the sink.

"Tara? Are you sick, should we go to the doctors?" asked Lily trying to process the scene.

"Come outside Tara, it's okay," I said, wiping her with a hand towel and bringing her into the kitchen.

"Guys…" Lily followed us.

"I'm so sorry," said Tara looking at me.

"Don't be; you have nothing to be sorry for," I said.

"What's going on?" asked Lily.

Both Tara and I were silent for what seemed like a long time.

"Ehm," I tried to form some kind of words.

"No. It's okay Amy, I've got this; Lily will understand," she said.

"Understand what?" asked Lily, "guys please just talk to me."

"I make myself sick," said Tara plainly.

"What…like purposely?"

"I've, I've got an eating disorder Lily; I'm sorry. I didn't want anyone to know, Amy found me one day; that's when I finally started to get better."

"What happened Tara? I thought the Wednesdays were working?" It sounded stupid to say; like a day could help such a serious condition.

"What are the Wednesdays?" asked Lily.

"It's this clinic place, I go every Wednesday and we just talk about coping mechanisms… The girls are all so lovely and they have been helping but…"

"But…" I urged her on.

"The exams coming made me more stressed than ever and well… Sam."

"Sam?" asked Lily, she looked uncomfortable in the situation. Maybe she did prefer not knowing what the real problems were and was better at just being there to help.

"I don't even understand it myself, I always say I blame my binging on exams and parents but I think I was fooling myself."

"But Sam?" I asked.

"You remember Chris right?" said Tara looking from me to Lily.

Lily looked confused. "Vaguely," she said.

I nodded. Of course I remember him.

"Well, I think that's what caused it."

The Real Reason Tara Got Sick

When I first moved to the same school as Tara, she had a boyfriend. One I didn't really know because of our distance. His name was Chris and he was two years older at seventeen. Tara had told me all about him during our weekend sleepovers; she whispered under the covers

"Oh Amy; you don't understand, he's like a whole other level of amazing."

I nodded, wide eyed and in awe. At the time I couldn't imagine a boy giving me any kind of attention, especially an older one. But Tara looked older than her age. She was curvy in a good way and had gotten boobs and a bum when we were only thirteen. Beside her I looked like a sad excuse of a teenage girl. All long limbed with no real features.

"And he's so mature," she said, "compared to all the other boys in our school. I mean don't worry, they're fine," she reassured me because at this stage we knew I was going to be moving next term.

"Oh I can't wait for you to meet him!" She sighed, "I'm sure you two will get on so well!"

"I'm so happy for you Tara," I said genuinely.

"Thanks Amy, what's great is that he doesn't..."

"He doesn't what?" I urged.

"Oh you know the way boys can be about girls who are... A little curvier..."

"You're gorgeous Tara!" I exclaimed, "All the boys must be crazy about you, you look so mature!" Tara was only a few

months older than me but I always felt like she was my older sister.

She shook her head. "It doesn't matter though, the only opinion I care about is Chris. The rest of them can think what they want."

"He sounds great," I agreed. "I can't wait to move next term and meet him."

I never did get to meet him because by the time I moved to their school he was gone. At the time Tara had told me his parents moved so he had to move with them and they were both heartbroken. Now, I knew the truth.

It was a weekday evening and Chris had asked Tara over to his house. She thought this was their relationship taking the next step. She had never been to his before. They were officially boyfriend and girlfriend and he had met her parents on numerous occasions but he had never brought her around. She dressed herself up in a black skirt and dark purple turtleneck. She even called me when she was getting ready to say how excited she was. After applying a small amount of mascara and lipstick, she left the house and followed the directions that Chris had text her.

When she arrived outside a high-rise block of apartments she wasn't too phased, most of London lived in apartments. She buzzed the buzzer and Chris answered, letting her in.

Once outside his door, she got butterflies. What if her parents thought her legs were too chubby to be wearing a skirt; or what if they disapproved of make-up. She smacked her lips together self-consciously; trying to make them less obvious but then Chris opened the door and behind him was eerily quiet.

"Hey," smiled Tara upon seeing him. God she did love looking at his face, his bone structure and stubble that wasn't yet there on the boys our age.

"Hello gorgeous," he grinned back beckoning her inside. She stepped in cautiously. The living room and kitchen were one open space and to put it plainly, the place was a tip. There were cigarette butts on the coffee table and empty bottles beside the couch.

"Ehm," Tara said awkwardly, "are you parents here yeah?"

"Nope," stalled Chris, "they've gone out for ehm dinner, ya know with some friends. A last minute thing, they really wanted *to meet you though. They told me to say hi," he added in at the end. Chris stepped towards her, Tara stomach began to do cartwheels; she was nervous. He took her face in his hand and kissed her, she kissed him back.*

Tara had told me, in whispers under our duvets, all of the things her and Chris had done.

"It's fun," she would whisper, "but I never let it get to that stage. I'm not ready for that and I'm far too young. He won't rush me though."

"Let's go to my room," said Chris pulling away from kissing Tara and leading her down the hall.

His room was messy, thought Tara, and the grey decoration really made the place feel dark and dreary.

"Nice room," she lied, sitting down at the edge of his bed.

"It does the job," smiled Chris. He sat back against his headboard and pulled Tara on to his lap so that her legs were on either side of him.

"Chris," Tara tried to say she wasn't ready for this; that she hadn't come here expecting this. Out of the corner of her eye she saw an open pack of condoms on his bedside table. She pulled out and tried to speak.

"Shhh," he whispered kissing her.

Tara let herself go, she liked Chris, she really did, she maybe even loved him she thought. And she liked being with him and doing stuff with him so why not take the next step. Tara knew why, she didn't mind Chris having a grope underneath her top, or up her skirt, but she knew at the back of her head what terrified her most about sex was the fact she'd have to let herself be seen.

"Let's take this off," whispered Chris through kissed and he started to pull Tara's turtleneck over her head. Tara hesitated but allowed her top to be taken off. Her skirt rested around her waist she thought so it mightn't be too bad. Her mind raced with thoughts of her skin piling over her hem. She shook the thought and kissed Chris.

Chris pulled back, Tara sat upright in shock.

"What, what is it?" she whispered terrified.

He shook his head, "Never mind, let's unhook this." He pulled her close and undid her bra, continued to kiss her. But Tara could feel his hesitance; something had changed.

He pulled out again and Tara crossed her arms over her chest self-consciously. Chris was looking down at his hands.

"Sorry Tara..."

"What Chris..."

"I can't, I didn't... I don't know I'm just not into this, I rushed into it I'm not feeling it...anymore," his voice trailed off.

Tara didn't know what to say, she was too embarrassed to get angry and too ashamed to get upset.

"Look we had fun, I just didn't realise you were so... Ehm..." He made rounded motion with his hands and Tara grabbed her turtleneck and pulled it over her head, forgetting about her bra she raced out of his apartment and down the stairs and ran all the way home without shedding a tear.

A few days later Tara told me Chris had moved away, now I knew he just never bothered to go to school much in the first place and had gotten a job.

Tara swore to herself she would never speak of what happened, that she would only let it make her stronger and she would file it away because she was the strong, brave girl who took no one else's shit and believed in herself wasn't she?

Now she told us that at the start of this year when Sam started to show her interest, she didn't believe he would keep it if he knew what she looked like without clothes on. Even if she had grown out of her chubby baby fat stage, she didn't see it herself. She still saw herself as the girl who was too grotesque to be looked at once she had her top off.

So she started to take control.

Chapter 16

Lily was completely shook that she didn't know; but she did say she was very oblivious to those kind of things. I think she was happier not knowing, but she tried her best. We stayed with Tara that night; her parents were away in Kent again, funny timing am I right?

"What are you going to do about Sam?" asked Lily; the next morning.

"Oh god, I don't know I'm so embarrassed. He's hardly still interested in me I've been such a bitch to him."

"I wouldn't be so sure," said Lily, "boys are pretty resilient. I think, you know if you're interested that it, that he would definitely still be."

I nodded in agreement, "as long as you think you're ready for it. He's not Chris Tara, remember that."

"I know he's not Chris; I just can't shake that… That awful; awful feeling; I mean guys to this day when I think of how embarrassed; how ashamed I felt…it still makes me sick." She shook her head.

"Don't; he was an idiot who didn't know how lucky he was," said Lily.

"Plus, he's probably a drug addict or something now; to be honest I'm glad you got out of that as quick as possible."

Tara laughed; "true I could have like three kids and live in some crappy little apartment at this stage."

I laughed but my stomach fluttered, kids, oh god how was I keeping this from them.

"Guys," I started, butterflies turning like crazy inside me. Was I really about to tell them?

"Yep," said Lily, sipping her tea casually.

"I… ehm… I."

"Spit it out," said Tara.

"I've the UTI again…" I blurted out before I could think. I was such an idiot.

We went to school together after breakfast. After assembly, Sam came straight up to Tara and the two of them went off talking, afterwards both Tara and he had two big smiles on their faces when they came into class together. Myself and Lily high-fived underneath the table; things were good. I was happy for Tara. But the white board was blurring, I didn't feel too good. When I walked to the next class everything went black for a second and I had to grab on to Lily's jumper for a minute until everything re-focused. I should go see Dr Foster later I thought as I sat down next to Lily in English.

"Are you okay?" she whispered.

"What?" I asked, barely hearing her. There was a loud banging somewhere, "can you hear that?" I asked.

"Hear what?" asked Lily… "Hear what Amy? What's wrong?"

Chapter 17

The light above me was so bright it was hurting my head. I opened my eyes and all I could see was white. For a brief moment I thought I was dead. I mean I knew my life was a disaster but it had always been better than the alternative. No, I wasn't dead; there were voices, informed, knowing voices echoing off the walls. I sighed and the room came into focus; a hospital bed, a ward, of course. I should have known.

"Waking up I see," smiled a young brunette who was suddenly leaning over me and adjusting some tubes that were leading into my left arm.

"Am I… Am I okay?" I asked, "Where's my mum?" She was the first person I wanted right now. The nurse smiled.

"You know, no matter how old you get, that's the first person anyone wants in times like these. I'll send her in." She walked away, after ticking off something on the clipboard at the end of my bed. I could hear all of the other patients around me, breathing and coughing, only separated by a sheet. Mum pulled mine open.

"Oh Amy, how are you?"

I was so glad to see her; as worried and frantic as she was. It seemed to me the most normal we'd been in months. I smiled.

"I feel fine but what happened? Is the baby okay?"

"Oh I'm sure she is, the doctors have tested all that. They think your blood sugar was too low. They're going to come and talk to you about that though. I told them, I keep telling her she's feeding two now." Mum threw her hands up in exasperation, "But anyways we will begin now. I told your dad, him and Mike have gone out to the groceries, I text them a big long list of everything healthy and yummy. We are going to feed you up no matter what!" I rolled my eyes at her.

"I'm sorry, I'll do better I promise," I said genuinely.

"Don't fret about it now Amy, we will figure it all out – someone's here to see you," said Mum suddenly looking worried. "It's Lily, she followed us here after you collapsed next to her in class."

I took in a deep breath. I knew this moment was coming. I couldn't keep this secret any longer; lying was so much harder than I'd ever thought, "It's time," I said. Mum nodded. She squeezed my hand and left the room.

A minute later Lily came bounding in.

"Oh my god I thought I'd got the wrong little room there for a moment! Imagine how awful that would be, some poor old man getting dressed." Lily giggled. I laughed and put my finger to my lips, pointing to next door, indicating how they could all hear us.

"Oops!" said Lily sitting down next to me, "Amy how are you, I was so worried. One minute you were fine and then whoosh, just like that." She made a falling motion with her hands. "What happened? I mean you were acting off all day."

"I'm fine Lil, it was low blood sugar or something."

"Oh thank god, Tara's on her way here in a mad hurry. But wait, why do you have low blood sugar, isn't that something diabetics get?"

"Yeah… well…there's something I haven't told you Lil…"

Her face dropped.

"Oh no, what is it? Please don't tell me you're really sick Amy, not you and Tara. Am I such a shit friend?"

"No Lily, I'm not sick and you're not at all a shit friend stop that… ehm I'm," I took a deep breath, this was harder than telling my parents for some strange reason.

"I'm pregnant."

Lily looked straight down at my stomach, which was still only slightly rounder than it ever was. I'd hidden it well and I was never going to be really big as Dr Foster said I was little and always would be. This was working in my favour.

"But what? No you're not. Stop it."   She paused. "I don't understand, how did this happen?" She asked not looking at me directly.

I laughed. "C'mon Lil," I said trying to make it more light-hearted. "You know exactly how it happened, it just wasn't meant to, is all."

She shook her head, 'no, no, no.'

"What is it? What's wrong?" I sat upright.

"I can't believe you would do this!" She stood up and was silent for a moment. "I mean what were you thinking? And then not telling anybody? I mean it all makes sense now, the baggy clothes, the fights with Luke," her voice faltered on the name. But she continued on, "But all of this secrecy? Amy, we're 17 I thought it was fucking stress! I mean Tara was a shock but this…"

"Lily please," I started, "calm…"

"No. Don't say a word. I don't think you've realised what you've done." She looked down at my normal stomach. "Does Tara know?"

I shook my head.

"If it's true then you're a fucking idiot Amy," she said before bursting into tears and walking out. I heard her screech something down the hall. I held my tiny tummy and tears started to fall. I had not expected that.

A head peeped around the curtain.

"Hey you, what's that all about eh? You finally slam her for hitting on Luke?" said Tara walking in and sitting at the end of my bed. I shook my head. If lily's reaction was like that, what on earth was Tara's going to be. I wanted it to be over already.

"I have to tell you something Tara."

"I know," she said looking straight at me. I looked back at her questioningly.

"I mean, I don't know what it is. But I know your keeping something from me. It's okay Amy, you can tell me."

She was being so her, so Tara, so understanding of even the things she didn't know. I was about to ruin that.

"I'm pregnant Tara," I whispered. She paused for a moment and her facial expressions changed but I couldn't read them.

"Oh thank god," she finally whispered back, looking relieved.

"Thank god?" I asked baffled.

She put up her hands, "I mean Amy I didn't know what to expect. I was terrified you'd become a drug addict and landed yourself here and then I thought because you were a drug addict you'd got wrapped up in some prostitution and gotten raped or had killed somebody. If you knew the things that have been racing through my mind these last few hours; well in all honesty

, compared to them being pregnant isn't as awful as it sounds," she smiled at me, "congratulations," she said.

"Tara, I didn't plan this. I don't want to be pregnant," I said dumbfounded by her response.

"Oh I know you didn't plan this but it happened didn't it, and normally when people get pregnant people congratulate them so I'm congratulating you. Also it makes us sound very old and mature so," she winked at me.

"Tara I don't know what to do," I said softly. She nodded.

"Why didn't you tell us?" she asked.

"I wanted you guys to all get your offers first. I know you've had them for a while now but it just got harder and you didn't need any distractions."

"I can't believe this," she said, "but I'm so glad you're not a hooker or a coke addict, wait you're not those also, are you?"

I laughed, "Of course not."

"Good now you better be ready to do some taking because I want to hear the whole story from start to finish." She shook her head. "I can't believe you've been able to keep this, it's actually crazy. But go on tell me everything, all the gory awful doctors looking up their visits too. And Luke oh my god does he know? Please." She put her hand over her mouth.

I laughed, "Yes he knows, he's actually been very good."

"Of course he has, he's an angel. Well, you know," she raised her eyebrows, referring to the Lily situation. "Nobody's perfect," she said, "and I don't believe he would have done anything with Lily to be brutally honest, he's so in love with you it's crazy."

I laughed.

"Okay go on then," she said, "I brought chocolate," she produced two bags of minstrels and tossed one to me. "Come on, start talking, and close your ears little baby," she whispered towards my stomach. "Boy or girl actually?"

"Girl," I smiled.

"Ahh how sweet, wow Amy, I bet you've gone through a lot."

I smiled at her and then I started to talk. I sat there with my best friend for hours and told her everything. Never had I felt such a weight lifted off my shoulders. Lies were terrible, lies made people lonelier than they ever needed to be. I knew that now.

Chapter 18
June

Things were bad. Things had never been worse and even though I had Luke and Tara and Mike; I had never felt so isolated.

I didn't go back to school after my visit to the hospital, there was only a week until exams and the doctors told me I needed to rest. I had tried texting Lily but no luck.

This was what my first day of exams went like.

"Oh Amy, hi," said two girls from my English class, pausing awkwardly in the hall to talk to me, I stalled; looking around me for someone to save me.

"Are you like… really?" asked the one called Sarah.

"Sarah, seriously, she means to say you know, it's crazy that you're like ya know… pregnant."

I looked at the two of them. The hall was filing up, 'Slut' I heard someone say but couldn't make out who it was a ripple of laughter rang through the hall. Sarah and the other girl, her name was Rose I think looked at each other and then turned away quickly.

"Well done," someone shouted from the bottom of the hall, I saw a group of boys laugh and heard murmurs of, "Poor Luke."

I started to feel really hot; there was no one I could see that I could talk to. I knew so many of these people but I realised now that we really know very few. Then there was a hand on my shoulder, "You okay Amy?"

I turned around, Sam was standing there looking at me.

"Yeah, yeah just…"

"People are idiots, come with me," he said grabbing my hand and bringing me into the examination hall.

"Amy, there you are," said Tara, the hall was pretty much empty. Filled with desks for each of us, she gave me a hug.

"I'm so sorry, I tried waiting out the front but when I didn't see you I thought you must already be in here."

"I came in the back," I said, "thought it would be easier that way…"

"People are such dicks," said Sam simply.

"Watch your language young man," said a voice; appearing behind us. It was Mr Longwood, our business teacher. We were all in that class together.

"Sorry sir," said Sam quickly.

"Why; might I ask, would one be referring to their peers in that manner," Mr Longwood always liked to speak in long terms and fancy words, I think he did it sarcastically most of the time.

"Just people being idiots," said Tara quickly.

"Yeah people giving poor Amy abuse," said Sam, oblivious.

"And why would that be?" asked Mr. Longwood, "Amy?"

"Oh it's nothing really," I said.

"You don't seem to be the kind of girl who would rub people up the wrong way?" commented Mr Longwood; obviously curious.

"Yeah, that would be me," Tara joked, trying to lighten the mood,

"I just think its bullshit," said Sam, "I mean if Luke were there he would have…"

"What's going on Amy? Does the school need to intervene?" asked Mr Longwood seriously.

"No; it's fine. Really, schools almost over everything will be fine," I said, smiling tightly.

Just then Luke walked into the hall.

"Amy, there you are. Lily just started screaming at me outside, I know you said she took it bad but…" His voice trailed off when he saw that Mr Longwood was standing with us.

"Hey Luke," said Sam and Tara in unison.

"Hello Luke," said Mr Longwood, he coughed. "Okay well looks like you kids have stuff going on, but don't let it affect your exams. English starts in twenty minutes." He put his hand on my shoulder, "ignore them kiddo," he said awkwardly before walking out.

"What was that all about?" asked Luke.

"Nothing," I said, "he just started asking questions, Luke everyone's talking about it, how did they all find out?"

"Lily," said Sam.

"What do you mean?" asked Tara, "there was no word of it last week when Amy was out."

"Apparently she told her old mate, you know Ally? They used to be close, yeah well what I heard from the guys was she told Ally at the weekend and well you know Ally."

"Can't keep her mouth shut," sighed Luke.

"Yep," nodded Sam. "I mean that's how I find out, I only heard this morning," he looked at me. "I hope you're, you know okay," he said.

"You too Luke, I mean you guys are crazy good at hiding this, the guys said it's been months."

"It has," said Luke.

"And you?' asked Sam turning to Tara.

"I've only known since last week," she said. "I couldn't tell you."

The two of them had been spending a lot of time together the past week or two, and I'd never seen her happier. I didn't think she was getting sick either.

"Yeah that's fair," said Sam.

"But what just happened with Lily?" I asked, remembering what Luke had first said.

"Oh shit yeah, I bumped into her outside the school. I was like okay I'll say hi, maybe she's chilled out now ya know?"

I nodded, Sam spoke, "Did Lily freak out when you told her or something? Is that why she told Ally 'cause I thought that was pretty weird of her, I mean I thought I knew Lily."

"So did we," said Tara.

I explained Lily's reaction to Sam.

"Holy shit, that's crazy, she's so chill usually."

"I know," said Luke, "so that's why when I said hey to her this morning I wasn't expecting her to start screaming at me about what an idiot I was, how this was terrible. I mean what did she want me to say?"

"I don't know, she's acting crazy," I said.

"I think a part of it could be that she didn't know, maybe she thinks I did. She hasn't talked to me since before the hospital and in school she literally just avoided me. Luckily, I had Sam," said Tara.

"Yeah, well I didn't even see her last week," said Luke. He had stayed at home to study; a lot of people did that in the last week.

"I'm sorry," I said, "I feel like I've caused this whole mess, I mean we were friends. We were all best friends."

"It's not your fault Amy, don't be silly," said Tara.

"She's being completely irrational," agreed Sam.

"You don't need her," said Luke.

Just then the bell rang and everyone started filing into the hall, I got so many looks and whispers. *People were so obvious*, I thought. It made me think about all of the times I've talked about people without actually knowing them or their situation and how I would never do it again.

Tara seemed to be thinking the same thing, *god I am never whispering again.*

"Come on," said Luke, "Let's go sit down."

"My desks over here," I said, we had assigned seats.

"I'm that way too," said Sam, "Row 11?" He asked.

"Yep, that's me, you're right behind me I think," I said.

"Great," said Luke, "look after her for me." He gave Sam a friendly pat on the shoulder. I gave Luke a look as if to say 'I don't need anyone looking after me, thank you' but I also thought it was sweet, so maybe it was a mixed look.

"Boys," said Tara, rolling her eyes, "Good luck," she whispered, heading towards her desk.

Sam and Luke had always been friends, but never super close. But I hadn't seen any of Luke's best friends say anything to him this morning so I had a feeling him and Sam were about to become good mates.

I walked with Sam to the other end of the hall, Lily walked by me; almost bumping into me. Our eyes met. She looked me up and down.

"Good luck Sam," she said, looking at him then.

Sam didn't say a thing, she walked away shaking her head.

I couldn't believe it, a week ago that girl was my best friend. Now she couldn't stand to speak to me. I couldn't help it, it made me feel like it was my fault.

"Just ignore it," said Sam, we were at our desks now, he was right behind me, "do your best, good luck."

"You too," I said my mind racing, but there was no time because the examiners were now here handing out papers. I did my best.

Chapter 19

The next few weeks were a blur; I felt like my stomach had just tripled in size. Even though it hadn't; the fact that now everyone knew made me think it must be obvious. Some people were nice, girls from classes came up to me and told me to ignore anyone being rude or mean and I appreciated them. But it was so hard, there can be so many good people and kind people but your mind will always fixate on the one bad, the mean words. People starred all the time, and whispered, some boys were being okay to Luke but mainly all of them felt awkward so they either made slut or whore comments to me from the safety of a group. Or they didn't say a word. Myself, Tara, Sam and Luke spent a lot of time together. Despite it all we had fun, neither Luke nor I felt judged by them and the four of us became even closer during those exam breaks and lunches.

I think I did okay, I mean I already had my offers and they were unconditional, meaning I had already gotten in on previous results so long as I didn't completely fail these I would be fine. On the last day of exams everyone was going to a big party in one of the boys' houses.

"I'm not going to go," I said to Tara at lunch on the last day.

"Yeah, I didn't think you would, are you sure though?" she asked.

"Yeah, I mean it wouldn't be enjoyable, plus I have never been so tired in my whole life," I laughed.

"I don't know how you're actually hiding it so well it's crazy."

'Oh no, it's there Tara is it not obvious?" I asked, holding my bump.

"Not at all, seriously."

"Thank god, it's these jumpers, I never thought I'd appreciate how awful they are," I said.

"They're pretty bad alright, but oh my god, this is the last day we will ever wear them? How crazy is that?"

"You know, with everything I had actually forgotten that this is the end. I'm kind of sad, I was always so happy here, Tara."

"You deserved to be," said Tara, "after the hell you went through beforehand." She was referring to all the bullying and lack of friends.

"This place became my second home; I mean it was amazing really. I had you and then Lily and Luke." I suddenly felt really nostalgic. This was the end of something so special in so many more ways than one.

"It's so sad about Lily," said Tara, "I mean I thought we were like sisters."

"Maybe she'll come around."

"Would you want her to? She was pretty awful to you Amy."

"I know but look, it's not worth losing such a friendship over is it?"

"You're right, nothing is," agreed Tara.

When I arrived home, that evening Mum, Dad and Mike were all in the kitchen; a rare sight for our busy family.

"Hey guys," I said, "what's going on?"

"We're going for dinner," said Mum.

"With Luke's family," added Mike, rolling his eyes.

"What?" I asked.

"Well I decided to call Sandy earlier, you and Luke finished your exams today and I know neither of you will be going out like all your friends. So I thought we would celebrate all together, plus, your father and I think all of us need to get together and talk about what's happening these next few months."

"Oh okay… you mean with the baby? Will you all be okay together, you don't really know each other?" I said.

"I know," said Mike, "it's going to be insanely awkward and weird."

"Mike stop it," said Dad, "we will be fine, we're going to be…" he coughed. "Family I guess… okay well get ready to go."

"Fine, fine, I'll just take of my uniform," I ran upstairs, thinking how insane my family were and how much they had changed since this all happened. Mum was insanely shy and would never before call a woman she didn't really know and Dad didn't like social outings with anyone other than his college friends. He also hated going out for dinner, full stop. I make them sound incredibly unsocial but really they just stuck to themselves and they liked Luke obviously but they were never the kind of parents who made him and his family a part of ours, Luke was my boyfriend not the families if that made sense. I threw on a pair of leggings because jeans did not fit and a big baggy jumper of Mike's.

We walked together to a local place and when we arrived Luke and his parents were already there.

Everyone exchanged awkward handshakes and hugs.

"This is so weird," Luke whispered to me, I nodded at him in agreement.

We ordered food and then there was an uncomfortable silence.

"So, I can't believe you two are finished," said Luke's dad after a moment.

"Crazy right," I said, sipping on my water.

"They're so grown up now," said Sandy looking at the two of us, a certain fondness in her eyes that gave me hope.

"More than we'd like," said Dad, he meant it as a joke I know but no one but Mike laughed.

"Sorry," said Dad immediately, "that came out wrong."

Mum looked embarrassed.

"Don't worry," laughed Sandy, "it's a new situation for us all."

"Thankfully,' added Luke's dad and this time we all laughed.

The ice broken, we talked openly over dinner about what we were going to do once the baby was born.

"Are you sure you're up for looking after the baby though Liz?" asked Sandy.

"I mean what choice do we have," said Mum. "I wouldn't want it to go to anyone else and I don't want Amy or Luke to miss out on their futures."

"We did talk about Luke taking a year out," said his dad, "we could support the two of them in raising the child."

"Yes but where and what happens when the year is over?" said Mum.

"She's right," agreed Sandy, speaking to her husband. "Luke and Amy have plans, I'm sure this is what a lot of families do right?" She looked to Mum. I noted that she seemed slightly in awe of Mum's calmness and the solid plan she had. I felt proud of my mum.

"It seems to be the best option, that way Amy and Luke will obviously still be involved but they can continue their futures."

"It won't be that long really," said Luke. "I mean in four years' time we will be done and we can get jobs and actually a proper place and..."

"Whoa young man," said his dad, as all our parents' eyes widened at his naïve future plans. I knew Luke thought all of these things would come true and even though I didn't actually believe in the future so much in the way he did. I didn't have the heart to tell him that, he was so good and positive how could I?

"What Luke means is," I said, "is that we have time, with this plan, we have time to figure out how and what's the best way to raise Alice."

"Alice?" they all asked. Luke and I looked at each other.

"That's the name we decided on," he said.

"It's pretty and simple. I once read a book with a girl called Alice in it and she was the most incredible person," I said.

"Just like our Alice will be," said Luke smiling.

"I've always liked Alice," said Sandy.

"It is sweet," agreed Mum. Our dads rolled their eyes.

"To Alice," said Mike, I had almost forgotten he was here, he raised up his glass.

"To Alice," we all said raising our glasses together.

Chapter 20
July

I got a new phone at the start of the summer holidays, I accidently dropped my old one into the toilet but that's a whole other story; but because I had a new phone; when I woke up one morning in the middle of July, a week before my birthday to a missed call from an unknown number I didn't think twice about calling them back.

It was Lily on the other end.

"Amy," she said, "its Lily."

"Lily," I said, sitting up slowly in bed, "ehm hi."

"I've messed up really bad," she was crying.

I stayed silent. I didn't know what she wanted from me.

"Can you come over?" she asked. I'm either a very weak or strong person because my first response was yes.

"Oh thank you Amy; I'm so sorry, for everything," said Lily.

"It's okay Lily but can you actually come here," I looked down at my stomach, I was due in less than two months and it had seemed like I became massive overnight. "I'm actually quite pregnant you know?"

We both laughed. "I'm on my way," said Lily.

I knew things weren't going to be okay straight away, but I knew had to at least try. I called Tara.

"What's up?" she said picking up, "it is like early."

"Lily's on her way over."

"What the fuck, how?" asked Tara, suddenly sounding very awake.

"She just called me, crying and talking about mistakes. Can you come over? I don't know what it's going to be like."

"God what the hell, yes of course, I've just gotta get up and shower but I'll be there as quick as I can."

"Great see you soon."

"Love you, bye." She hung up. I got up and got myself slightly dressed. These days that means tracksuits and baggy tops, more like pyjama wear than anything else to be honest. I washed my face and the doorbell rang. I heard Mum answer it.

"Ehm Amy," she called urgently up the stairs. I should have told her Lily was on her way, she knew all about how we hadn't talked in weeks.

"It's okay, Mum," I said coming out of bedroom and on to the landing, from where I could see Lily standing in my hall, looking out of place.

"Hey Lily," I said calmly, "come on up."

"You're okay Amy?" asked Mum as Lily started up the stairs.

"I'm perfect," I said. Lily hugged me when she reached me. I hugged her back cautiously. We walked into my room and sat on my bed. I thought she was about to start talking about the ignoring and maybe even apologise for telling everyone.

"Amy," started Lily.

"Yeah?" I said.

"I had sex," she said, her lip quivering.

"Oh…" I was speechless.

"And I know I've been terrible to you and I'm sorry but then this happened and I didn't know who to turn to."

Okay, there was my apology. It seemed to be the most I was going to get at this stage.

"I'm so sorry Amy, I should never have told anyone and I shouldn't have freaked out the way I did, I mean the whole thing still…" she looked down at my stomach, "it still freaks me out a bit but I was a bitch and I'm so sorry."

"It's okay," I smiled and tried to ignore the fact that me being pregnant 'freaked her out'.

"So what the hell happened!" I asked.

She put her head in her hands, it looked like she was crying.

"Hey, hey what's wrong Lily?" I said, moving closer. There was a knock on my door and Tara walked in.

"Well isn't this a sight," she said simply. "I didn't think you'd be the one crying." She gave Lily daggers.

"Hey Tara," said Lily, looking up.

"Well, what's going on," she asked looking at me.

"Everything's okay, Lily apologised. I think things just got out of hand right?" I looked at Lily, trying to send her brain signals to also say sorry to Tara.

"I'm sorry Tara; I was terrible to you too. I shouldn't have ignored you and oh god I shouldn't have snapped at Luke," she started to cry again.

"You're forgiven but quit sobbing and tell us what the hell is going on."

"She had sex," I said plainly and the three of us looked at each other. This was our friendship; messy, honest and very complicated; but at least we were real. We were glad to be back together. So for a moment we laughed, but then that moment passed and Lily burst back into tears. Tara sat on the other side of her and we both hugged her.

"Shh little one, tell us what happened, we won't be mad," she said.

"Are you sure you're not mad?" she asked.

"Of course we're sure, we're a team us three, we can't let anything get between us okay," I said.

"Okay," said Lily 'well I didn't expect to feel like this afterwards," she said.

"After sex or after the fight?" asked Tara

"Who was it?" I asked.

"Joshua and after the sex," said Lily, sitting back in my bed, she had stopped crying and wiped her eyes. "It only happened a few days ago, two nights ago at that party, you know Ally's?"

"Oh that bitch," said Tara, I slapped her softly.

"Yeah she actually is, god I'm such a terrible friend I should never have told her but she found me crying in the bathroom; I was just so upset over how I'd reacted and …"

"It's alright, it doesn't matter anymore," I said.

"Continue with Joshua, what happened?" pushed Tara.

"Well, you guys know I wanted to 'do the deed'," she put up her hands to make exclamation marks as she said this, "and well Joshua was there and he was flirting with me…. or at least I think he was…"

"He definitely was Lily, you're just oblivious most of the time," I laughed.

"Well he was super touchy and stuff, so I took that as a good sign. Was I right to take that as a good sign yeah?"

"God bless your innocence," said Tara shaking her head, Lily never failed to make us laugh with her naivety around boys. It was funny too because she could be such a flirt but she would have no idea she was actually flirting.

"You were right to," I laughed.

"Okay so, well we kissed in the garden; there was a load of people there so it wasn't weird…"

"Continue," said Tara. Lily grimaced.

"Then we went inside to get more drinks and I said I needed to go to the bathroom; so I went upstairs and when I came out of the toilet he was there waiting for me."

"Ohh," both Tara and I said, "keep going."

"I was just like hey whatever, and he goes found you and here's your drink, so he passed me a beer and we both just stood kind of in the hall chatting for a bit until you know; we started kissing again…but this time it was more."

"Full on," said Tara, Lily nodded.

"Then a bedroom door next to us opened and out came like who was it, Sarah and Kevin or something, she was so pissed and was like oh my god Lily here's a free room."

I cringed and so did Tara but we tried to keep our faces straight; we knew what was coming.

Lily exhaled, "Of course Joshua took me by the hand and brought me in and of course; me being me, followed and well at the time I was excited you know and … well I wanted to and I still do I mean I don't regret it I just feel so weird…"

"What kind of weird?" I asked gently.

"Like I'm not just me anymore, like I let him see more of me than I was ready to let anyone see or do."

I nodded. "Whoa," said Tara, "I mean, was it good?"

"It was; it actually was but just the next day I woke up and felt like absent. I haven't been able to shake it, Amy did you feel like this?"

"I'll be honest with you Lil I didn't; but I love Luke and I loved him when we did it… Or at least I think I loved him; maybe it was too early to know, or maybe we never really know… but I didn't feel like that. After I did I felt bigger, more whole."

Lily shook her head, "I'm an idiot. I should have waited."

"Hey don't worry," said Tara, "one of us had to do the cliché hook up in a bedroom at a party right."

Lily smiled. "I suppose so, do you think it'll go away? This feeling I mean."

"Of course it will," said Tara. "I promise you, I've felt like I've given away myself before to people who didn't deserve me and it does feel empty and strange, I know what you mean. But it will stop, you'll realise that you're more than the people you've let be with you, and you can have a clean slate, you can be fresh again. Hell, babe, you can even be a virgin again, virginity is pretty much a social construct anyways. Everyone considers sex differently, some things feel more intimate to one than they do to another, so you can always have a clean slate. "

I thought Tara must be talking about Chris and how he must have used her; I'd never thought of it like that, it's funny how you know people and you know what goes on with them but you never know fully how things make them feel.

"I've really missed you guys," said Lily, pulling us in. "I promise to never screw up again."

"Ah I'm sure you will… but won't we all?" laughed Tara.

She was almost crying at this stage.

"Pancakes?" I said from the neck of Lily's arm.

"Pancakes," they both said in unison and off we went. We all ordered double because it wasn't fair that only I got to eat for two.

Chapter 21

"Happy Birthday to you, happy birthday to you, happy birthday dear Amy; happy birthday to you." Luke was the first person to call me at twelve p.m. on the dot.

I laughed after picking up the phone to hear him singing down at me.

"Finally an adult," he said, "I am so happy and proud of you; I'm coming over in the morning with cake."

"You're an idiot," I said, "the last thing I need is cake, I look like an elephant."

"You're pregnant stop it," he laughed, "and if it's any condolence you make a beautiful elephant."

I laughed, "You're just trying to make up for the fact that you've been away all week with the boys."

"That may or may not be true, was that really bad of me. I did think I shouldn't."

"I'm joking Luke, of course you should have, the girls have been with me every day; everything's the way it used to be with us."

"That's great Amy; I know we'd probably be in Italy all together right now if this hadn't happened so I promise you're going to have a great birthday."

"Italy was a flop trip anyways, thanks Luke, how was the week with the boys after all? Everyone cool with you again?"

Some of Luke's friends had kind of been avoiding him since word got out, but Sam had organised the trip so of course he went.

"Yeah like totally chill again, I think they were just freaked out but now; now they're really cool with it all, I'm relieved to be honest. I mean I know I probably won't see them next year but if I don't get into Edinburgh; well you never know."

"I know, better to be on good terms with everyone and you will get in of course," I said, "now I am dead tired so let me sleep but I love you."

"Can't wait to see you tomorrow birthday girl, love you."

I clicked off the phone and fell asleep.

When I woke up there was more candles and cake, this time it was my family surrounding my bed.

"It's way too early for this," yawned Mike; holding a bouquet of flowers.

"Mike," said Mum, grinning from ear to ear, "You're eighteen," she said to me.

"I agree," I said to Mike and then to Mum, "crazy I know."

They started to sing and Dad walked in with a cake.

"Breakfast is served," said Dad, putting the vanilla frosted pile of deliciousness in front of me.

I sat up and they all sat down around me.

"You're an adult now," said Mike, "think of all the things you can do without hiding them."

I laughed and Dad shot him a look before relaxing and laughing himself.

"You kids are going to give us heart attacks one of these days, did you hear Mike come home last night?" asked Mum.

Mike went red.

"What no?" I said, grinning, good my baby brother was finally breaking the rules.

"Yeah exactly that's the problem, neither did I so I presumed he was at Liam's but then I find him in his bed this morning, lord knows where he was' she looked at Mike urging him to tell her."

"I was just with the guys, you know the usual. You know where I go don't you Amy?"

"Yeah of course I do," I lied, "don't worry, Mum, they're boys, luckily they're much more immature than girls." I gave her a wink.

"Oh lord, I don't even want to think," she sighed.

"Then don't, eat cake and have fun." I took a bite. Mum smiled.

"I know we're hard on you Amy, we have to be but your father and I are proud of you. Aren't we?"

Dad nodded, "Of course we are."

Mike rolled his eyes and went for a second slice. I heard a knock at the door, followed by footsteps and laughing and suddenly there was Luke, Lily, Tara and Sam all standing at my door.

"Happy Birthday," they shouted excitedly, holding gifts and sweets.

"Come in come in," said Mum and her and Dad got up, leaving us to it. Mike stayed.

"We've got to sing guys come on sing," said Tara jumping up and down at the bottom of my bed like a little kid, I laughed.

"Guy's I'm still in my pyjamas, I look awful," I said as Lily snapped a photo of me surrounded by my gifts.

"Here," said Tara pulling out a tiara and a pink birthday girl banner for me to wear, she placed them over me.

"Beautiful," she clapped her hands together and everyone laughed. Luke came over to me and handed me a small box.

"Just something little," he said and everyone rolled their eyes. Luke had never done 'little' presents. Yeah, he was that guy.

"Aw thank you," I said.

"Now, now, don't get soppy on us, open the damn thing you've more to get," said Lily.

I untied the gold ribbon and opened the box, inside was a small gold rectangular frame on a keychain. On the top part of the little frame was an old small Polaroid of me and Luke when we first started going out, we were sitting side by side on the wall of our school and making a face at each other, I remember the photo being taken by Tara but I didn't think Luke still had it, underneath was a blank space, the size of a small photograph.

"It's for the baby, when it comes we can put in a photo of it, so that no matter what happens or where we go we will always all be together with you, I thought we could give it to her then when she got old enough."

I had tears in my eyes, but I was just hormonal right. I wiped them away.

I could see Lily was on the verge too, even Tara looked melancholy.

"Thank you so much, it's beautiful Luke I really love it, thank you."

He just smiled and for a moment everyone was silent.

"Time for more presents I think," said Sam brightly.

"I'll go get mine," said Mike running off, when he came back we were all sitting on my big bed in a circle opening presents. I got photo albums and scrapbooks made by Tara and Lily, notebooks and books from Sam, he'd remembered conversations we'd had over the year about authors I'd liked, I thought it was really sweet. Mike's present was incredible. He'd made a fold out book of photos, all since I'd gotten pregnant. I hadn't seen him take them but there were ones of me and Mum and Dad having conversations at the kitchen table, of me leaving in the morning, he was a sneaky little photographer but they were beautiful, there was even one of me and Luke standing outside, looking in depth in conversation. He had added quotes to the back of them, words we had said and memories, I laughed at how he had scrawled vegetarian lasagne on the back of the first one, that was when I told them. Then there were 'sometimes we need to be scared a little to realise how lucky we are'.

"Dad said that didn't he?" I asked and Mike nodded. Everyone was leaning in to look at it with me.

"That's a terrible dress though?" asked Tara reading out the back on one. I looked to Luke 'that day' I said and he laughed.

"It really was," said Mike.

"Ah…" said Luke pulling a face.

The rest of them looked confused and I realised they didn't even know about the almost abortion. *Not now*, I thought.

"Just a terrible fashion choice," I said to them, they nodded; I made a lot of them.

"Mike this is amazing," I said, he shrugged embarrassed.

"It really is," said Luke.

"Thank you so much," I pulled him into a big hug, he went red.

"Group hug," yelled Lily and they all joined in.

"Okay, okay, suffocating myself and little person here," I laughed after a few minutes we all let go but no one moved. We stayed there just like that for most of the day, and we talked and laughed and listened to each other. The room got dark and we turned on the fairy lights and ordered Chinese. It was the best birthday I'd ever had.

The Worst Birthday I Ever Had and Something You Don't Know About Me

"You're gorgeous," he said looking straight at me, "when did this happen?"

I blushed, but not as much as I would have had I been sober.

"Seriously Amy, how had I never seen you like this before," he placed his hand on my waist, running his fingers up and down.

"I..." I was about to tell him I had a boyfriend. But this was Ethan Buell, a senior from my old school, someone who had laughed at me in the hallways growing up. I know it shouldn't have mattered who he was, I know I should have been stronger, but I had my weaknesses. Luke and I had been going out only a few months, it was the night of my sixteenth birthday and this eighteen year-old-boy who had once mocked me wanted me.

"Can I get you another drink," asked Ethan.

"I'm okay," I said, holding up my beer to him.

"So where did you disappear to?" he asked and I told him about my new school.

"Why are you here?" I asked, referring to the party we were both standing in the middle of. Lucy, in my year was also turning sixteen, me and the girls went out for dinner ourselves for mine last night and had decided to come here tonight, Luke was away with family for the weekend.

"Lucy's my cousin," he said, wrapping his other hand around my waist and pulling me into him. I flinched and looked around. It was late and most people were past remembering tiny details of who was with who. But I knew everyone around me and everyone knew Luke.

I obviously knew it was wrong. I was trying to hide it for god's sake.

"Not here," I whispered, which of course Ethan took as a great invitation for more.

"Come with me," he said, taking my hand. I let him.

I followed him up the stairs and into a bedroom and I let him kiss me up against the closed door, I let him lead me to the bed and I kissed him back. I didn't let it go any further but it didn't matter. I had cheated and the worst thing is, while I was doing it I knew it was wrong.

I know why I did it, you probably do too. And it certainly doesn't make it okay.

I did it because after years of abuse, of hurt and of feeling ugly and unloved, I felt like I had control over someone who had hurt me. In the mess of the night, Ethan represented to me all of the people who had bullied me in that school and by kissing him I was suddenly worthy. It was so stupid. A part of me was also excited but how much my life had changed since my fifteenth birthday which I'd spent alone in my pyjamas, watching re runs of Friends and trying not to cry about my lack of them. Sounds funny when I say it like that but it was a dark time.

But then on the bed with Ethan I remembered that thing's we're different now, I did have friends and I didn't need to prove myself to people any longer, especially when I had someone like Luke who loved me.

"I've got to go," I said to Ethan, getting up off the bed.

"Why, don't leave now Amy."

"No, my mum's here," I lied, "I'm sorry."

I raced away from the party. It hadn't fulfilled me. it hadn't taken back all of those words those people had said to me and it certainly hadn't healed the wounds those words left, at the end of the day I had just made myself a worse person. I didn't feel the freedom of being young and reckless at sixteen. I felt sick. I called Luke; without thinking, I just did what my mind was telling my body to.

He picked up on the first ring.

"Hey Amz," he said quietly, I could tell he was in bed.

"Luke," I said quickly, "I've done something terrible."

"What, what's going on are you okay?" he asked quickly, suddenly alert.

I took a deep breath and started walking in the direction of home.

"I kissed someone," I said. Silence.

"I kissed someone and I wasn't too drunk to not know, you probably don't want to know who he was but it might explain it better," I said.

"No," said Luke quietly.

"Luke I'm so sorry, I'll explain," I started to cry.

"No don't," he said simply, "I don't want to know who he is."

"Luke, it was so stupid, and I know this isn't going to change what I just did but Luke I love you. More than anything in the world and I can't believe what I've done."

"Was it for a reason?" he asked calmly, he wasn't mad, his voice was even.

"Well yes, but no reason is good enough, Luke I understand if you can't forgive me but please, please believe me when I say there's nobody more important than you and –"

"I forgive you Amy," he said quietly.

"What, really?" I was almost home and my tears were stopping.

"Amy, we make mistakes. I know you're a good person and I love you. I believe you when you tell me it's for a reason but I'm not ready to hear what that is because that means knowing who he is and I just don't want to know that yet. But one day okay."

"Okay," I said, "Luke; are you serious?"

"Yes I am Amy, we're okay, are you home now?"

"Just outside home," I said.

"Okay, well go to bed, I'll be home tomorrow, let's talk then."

"I love you," I said.

"You too," he clicked off and sank into my front steps in shock. It was a cold summers night but I'd hardly felt it.

I knew why Luke forgave me, it was because his older sister had told him that weekend that she had cheated on her boyfriend of four years but it had been for a reason. He wouldn't tell me what it was but her boyfriend had understood that people are only human and perfection isn't reality.

I still felt like a terrible person for a while but in the end it made me more open to peoples mistakes, Luke made them throughout our relationship, nothing like cheating but mistakes still and I could see past them. I haven't told you those mistakes because I don't dwell on them and I know once someone hears about the mistakes a person makes it's easy to see them for only that. But that's not who Luke or I are or anyone for that matter, no one is there mistakes. So yeah, you were probably wondering why I was so okay so quickly with him and Lily, well this is why. I'd already done it to him a long time ago, I knew we were young and I knew we did bad things but I knew that didn't make us bad *people. And I knew our loves was stronger than a few wrong turns and a couple of mistakes. What made me and Luke perfect was that we weren't perfect at all, not one bit. And we weren't blind to the fact that we made mistakes either nor in denial that we made them, we were just in love and when you're in love you see more, so in a round-about way, you're willing to see less.*

Chapter 22
August

It was the third of August; I ticked of the day on the calendar in my kitchen like I always did. Today we got our exam results and on this day in a month's time I would have a baby.

"Will you be okay?" asked Mum from the kitchen table, "going in and getting your results I mean."

"Yeah of course, Tara is going to collect me on the way with Sam and Lily and Luke will both be there, I'll be fine," I smiled and took a spoonful of cereal.

"I'm sure you did fine, you've got your offers from London University anyways, if you don't get the exact marks you've still got a shot at a different course so don't stress okay."

I rolled my eyes, she was more stressed than me, honestly the last thing I'd thought of this summer was results. I'd spent time with the girls and Luke and Sam, we'd gone to the beach for a day last week when the sun was blaring, I'd been to the centre for young women so many times but still no sign of Crystal. Deborah was helping me look, that reminded me

"Oh Mum I said I'd pop over to Deborah and the girls at the centre this afternoon after I got my results, they all want to know how I get on."

"That's sweet; I'll have to meet all of these girls one day."

"Yeah, I think the girls might come with me, they're kind of curious too and Deborah is always telling me to bring people."

"Good idea, well, all of you can come back here this evening and I'll cook your favourite."

I laughed and Mum looked confused, my phone pinged 'here x' from Tara. I kissed my mum on the forehead.

"Thanks Mum, I'll text you, see you later Tara and Sam are outside."

"Tell them I said good luck," she called after me.

"Hey guys," I said, hopping slowly into the back. I was only getting bigger and bigger.

"You good back there partner' asked Tara.

"Doing my best," I joked.

"Hey there Amy," said Sam pulling away from my house.

"Thanks for the lift," I said.

"No problem, are you nervous?" he asked.

"I am, extremely," said Tara wringing her hands nervously.

"But…" I started.

"I know, I know I won't be using my results with theatre school but still I don't know why but I've got all these butterflies ah," Tara had gone for the audition and gotten a definite offer. She was in.

"You'll do great," said Sam putting his hand on hers. They were cute, in a non-showy way. Sam and Tara were slow and steady, small displays, Tara was happy and so was Sam.

"What about you Sam, do you think you got enough for social studies?"

"I mean, I hope so but you never know right, I've a few back-ups anyways."

We pulled up outside the school, everyone in our year was walking in excitedly. Some with their parents, some in groups of friends. I hadn't thought this through.

"I can't walk in there," I said. Sam and Tara turned around to face me. "No I mean I really can't. I'm an idiot I didn't think this through, I did think it might be awkward but I forgot completely about parents and…"

"No, shh Amy, you don't have to do this but you can. I know you can."

I looked at her, then looked out the window, there was Sarah and her posse, near her was Ally with both her mum and dad.

"Oh god," I groaned putting my head in my hands.

"I think people will admire you if you do," said Sam, "I know I would."

"Yeah Amy they really would and you know what, anyone who gives you a look is just full of shit. Honestly and you will never see these people again, you may as well go out with a bang."

I couldn't help but smile and think to myself 'literally', "You guys go in, I'll call the school or something."

There was a tap on my window Luke, he was beaming.

I opened the door and he put his head in to all of us

"I got in guys I got Edinburgh!"

"Oh my god Luke well done," I cried and wrapped my arms around his neck. I was so happy for him, this was his dream. Away from me and the baby I know…

"But what's even better is I got London too," he said looking at me, "I'll be able to stay."

"What really?" Luke had applied to Edinburgh because the points were lower but in the process he had fallen in love with the place, I just presumed it would have been his first choice.

"Well done mate," said Sam.

"Yeah congratulations Luke really well done," smiled Tara, "come on let's go find out our futures," she said.

"I'll help you out," said Luke taking my hand, I hesitated.

"What's wrong?" he asked. Sam and Tara looked at me.

"Nothing," I said and took his hand to get out. If people were going to talk about me I may as well give them something to talk about.

When we walked into the hall, Lily was the first person I saw. She was talking with a group of people and she looked really happy. The group she was with saw me as I walked in and she turned with them. She said something quickly and ran over to me. I breathed a sigh of relief and I think Tara did beside me too, we shouldn't have doubted her but the past isn't easy to forget even if you can forgive.

"Girls," she said seriously grabbing our hands, "I got it I got my first choice," we both hugged her and screamed before going to the table to get ours.

I got it; I got nursing in London University. When I opened the envelope and saw it I felt nothing, I know that's not good sign but with everything else, what I got in my exams honestly seemed like the least important thing ever, and I just didn't feel the same attachment to nursing as I once did. I knew that it was my future but what was my future now anyways? I tried to shake the feeling.

"Well…" Tara and Lily looked to me nervously.

"Huh? Oh yeah I got it, first choice," I tried to smile.

"Oh well done Amy, I don't know how you've done everything," said Lily and Tara hugged me.

"Me too, first choice I mean, not that it matters, but if I have some incredibly personality change overnight then I'll be in pre-med in the morning, wouldn't my parents be delighted," she laughed.

"I think you'll have much more fun keeping them on their toes with you in acting school," said Lily.

Sam and Luke walked over to us.

"I think she just loves the fact that it's out of their control," laughed Sam.

"So true," said Lily rolling her eyes, "nah I make them sound worse than they are, they are happy for me with whatever I do but you know…"

"It's fun to feel rebellious," I said.

"Exactly," she said and we all laughed, I looked around. Some people were looking over but mainly everyone was much more concerned about their own futures. I shouldn't have thought about it so much, at the end of the day, people are always a lot less interested than you actually think.

We made a quick escape; I wasn't too keen in sticking around in case a few teachers wanted to talk. Tara was the same, their star med student wasn't talking her offer; stats would be down.

So Lily, Tara and I all piled into the back of Sam's car with him and Luke sitting in the front.

"So guys, where to?" asked Sam.

"I think we're going to head over to Amy's pregnant place aren't we?" said Tara enthusiastically.

"Pregnant place," I blurted out laughing, Lily joined me. "Yeah it's just where Amy goes when she feels like being pregnant," she said.

The boys laughed, "I'm sorry," said Tara putting her hands up, "but you all knew what I meant, clinic or whatever it is."

"Well, to the pregnant place we go," said Sam, stepping on the accelerator.

On the way I texted Mum to let her know I got my place, I didn't feel the excitement I knew she was feeling when I received back,

'Congratulations you are a star' followed by rows of emojis, she loved those. But I packed those feelings away as we pulled up outside my little renovated church.

"This is it," I said and Sam stopped the car. "There should be a group in there right about now and I told them you all were coming so don't worry, they often bring people for support, it's pretty chill."

We all hopped out of the car, Lily looked uncomfortable, she linked her arm in with mine and I led the way.

Inside, everyone was in a circle with Deborah standing up and walking around talking expressively to the girls.

"Hey guys," I said loudly and they all turned and smiled.

"Amy," cried Deborah, "you brought your friends; we were all just talking about when you would arrive."

Katie stood up and came over to me, she was the girl who was considering getting an abortion on my first day here. She had done it but she still came to visit. We had gotten friendly. She was a really fun person to be around. She gave me a hug.

"Come and sit down guys," she said to all of us.

Deborah nodded, "Yes do, tell us all your story, don't worry you don't need to be pregnant to have one."

All the girls laughed, I did too. Lily had unhooked her arm from me and was shifting nervously from foot to foot. Tara just looked in awe of everyone. Luke and Sam both walked over to the seats pretty relaxed and sat down, I was about to take a seat next to Luke when Lily let out a cry.

"Lily calm down," I saw Tara whisper furiously into her ear, she started to shake.

"I've got to go," said Lily, "you guys, you're just…" She looked nervous but angry.

"Lily what's wrong?" I asked, walking over to her at the edge of the circle.

All the girls started to whisper 'is she okay?' I heard one say 'is it us?' said another 'if it is what a bitch, how is Amy friends with her'

"Lily you're really causing a scene," said Tara.

Lily froze, she had gone very pale and looked like she was going to get sick.

"Is she okay?" asked Deborah, walking quickly over to us

"Lil'." I reached out to her. She slapped me away. She looked at all of the girls sitting in a circle and suddenly I saw what she saw. Wasn't it what I saw on my very first day? However, unlike Lily I had the fact that I was one of them. I hated

131

myself for seeing them that way when I knew them now and I didn't know if Lily would ever be able to change her way of thinking. She was traditional that way.

Her face scrunched up, I knew she was seeing the girls in crop tops that showed off their pregnant bellies and the dirty tracksuits and greasy high ponytails. I knew she couldn't see past this to the good, to even Jules in her nurse's uniform or Abby wearing her office clothes.

"Lily just take a breath okay, we can-"

"No Amy, it's okay. I can't, I'm just not a good enough person I guess I should have known. I'm going and I'm sorry I just….. I don't know if I can' she raised her hands and I knew she was talking about more than just being here, at the centre. She was referring to our friendship. There were tears in her eyes.

"I'm sorry, I do hope everything works out okay but I can't pretend that I don't just see a mess up when I look at you now, I know I shouldn't but I do. I'm sorry…" She turned and started to walk quickly away.

"This is it Lily," yelled Tara moving after her. I pulled her back as Lily turned around. Tara continued, "You don't get another chance, if you walk out now it's the end."

Lily just stared back. I stayed rooted to the spot. A mess up. I had really lost Lily this time, I knew there was no going back.

"You're choosing this," said Lily 'and that is what I can't watch. Some people have no choice in what happens to them Amy' I knew she was referring to her sister. In a way I understood. Lily walked out. Tara let out a cry and turned to me. Luke and Sam stood up, for a few moments there was silence. Then of the girls spoke, Rachel was her name.

"Well that was the most drama we've had in a while," they all nodded in agreement.

"And I mean we've had our fair share of drama here, didn't expect it to be your friends though," said Katie.

"We're not all like that," said Tara wiping her eyes.

"Are you okay?" asked both Luke and Sam to Tara and I. We looked at each other.

"Maybe something else is going on with her," I said, "like do we really know, she can't be acting so-"

"Oh my god Amy, you are so in denial," cried Tara. I stepped back. That was not what I was expecting.

"She isn't able for it okay," said Tara, "she's been an absolute bitch to you and you continue to forgive her and then when she's mad or angry at you, you mope."

"I don't mope…"

"Yes, yes you do and you stress so much about her. Why? You don't need her, can you not see, can you not see that all this time you've had me… is that not enough?"

"Oh Tara, of course it is; I just thought I should try…"

"It's not your problem she can't deal with small twists in life. I just don't like to see you upset because of one person when you've so many others."

"I've you Tara, thank you so much," I shook my head at myself. Maybe sometimes not letting someone back in was the stronger option.

"She's right," said one of the girls, we both looked up; they were all still sitting their smiling. It was like we had just put on one long performance.

"So many people left me," said Jenny.

"Me too, even my boyfriend hah," laughed another.

"It's part of the package," nodded Katie.

"It's tough," said Deborah as we sat down, Luke and Sam were still standing in shock. 'But what you learn is who is really there for you and Amy. You seem to have a solid bunch around you."

I looked to Tara. "I do," I said.

"But thank you for the drama," said Jenny. "I don't remember a scene like that since this girl Lulu's mother came in screaming at her because she's just found out the father of Lulu's baby was her own boyfriend."

"God yeah that was a battlefield," said another.

"Did that actually happen?" asked Sam innocently.

"Of course," they laughed, "but don't worry the boyfriend was closer in age to Lulu than he was to the mother, it was a messy situation, everyone felt bad for Lulu."

"So this happens a lot?" asked Luke. "I mean people just ditch their friend because they're pregnant?"

"God of course!" said one of the girls.

"It's like a rite of passage, some people lose all of their friends but you know then they find us."

"What we do is," said Deborah, "we concentrate on the people that are in our lives rather than the people who are gone or who have left, we choose to put our energy and love into those who will return it, there's many people in this world and we can waste time being sad about the one or the few who can't return our love or," she paused for effect, I reckoned she would be an actress or performer in another life, "or we can choose to love what we have, and be thankful for them."

"That's really lovely," said Tara, I nodded.

"You're right, thank you all so much, if it weren't for all of you I would be a hell of a lot more in pieces than I am right now…but you know what, screw that," the girls nodded.

"Screw anyone who doesn't accept us for what we do and who we are."

The girls started to clap and I began to laugh, Tara laughed next to me.

"Right then," smiled Deborah, "I think that wraps us up for the day."

Chapter 23

It was weird, when I looked at myself in the mirror I still saw the seventeen-year-old me. Because for most of being seventeen I wasn't pregnant, I was just me, normal, slim, blonde. I still saw that, or at least when I thought of myself that was the image I got. Was that just wishful thinking, would I ever be the same again after this baby was born.

I looked at myself in the mirror, up close. *No*, I thought, there was already a difference in me. I could never go back. I sighed and went downstairs, slowly. There was only a few days left to my due date left. I found Mum in the living room going through my university letters and information. I forced myself to act excited.

"Oh Amy come look, you can take these extra modules if you choose later on to change isn't that great? Everything so much more open these days."

She passed me a leaflet as I sat down. "Ooh great, it's so close," I said.

"Well September 23rd is induction week. The baby will all be settled and happy by then. I'm glad we did that big shop the other day, at least now we have all its clothes and crib for the first while."

"All new people," I said, ignoring her reference to our baby shopping day. It had been somewhat fun picking out clothes and cribs, even a pram but it had all felt so weird. "Won't next year be crazy, I'll have to make all new friends."

"You're great at making friends," said Mum, I gave her a look.

"Oh honey, that was years ago at this stage. You're a completely different person and besides it was never you, it was them."

"I know that now, I don't know though, I'm actually really nervous… I really am, Mum."

"My god she's human," laughed Mum.

"What?" I asked confused.

"All this time Amy, all you've gone through in these last few months is enough to turn most people upside down. But you, you've been the calmest person in it all and it's been happening to you. I don't know how you've done it and I'm very proud of you, all you had to be scared and frightened of, an abortion, a boyfriend and my god a baby in a few days but you don't falter. It's okay Amy, you're allowed to be scared," she put her arm around me.

"The thing is, Mum, the pregnancy doesn't make me nervous anymore and I don't know why…" I was about to tell her I was afraid I was making the wrong choice, going to college to study nursing, despite the baby.

"Maybe it hasn't kicked in yet, maybe when you've a screaming baby in your arms you'll realise," she joked.

I smiled, "Maybe but Mum, what makes me most nervous… or not nervous so much as I think it's wrong, I don't know if I want to…" but I couldn't finish my sentence because I felt something weird, something like a pop. I looked down.

"Mummmm," I cried out.

"Oh my god oh my god," she jumped up, "MIKE CALL YOUR FATHER, AMY'S WATER BROKE."

I stayed looking at my soaked pants. This was happening. Mike ran into the living room and looked at me.

"Oh shit," he said.

"Mike, language," said Mum. I managed out a small laugh, "call your father and tell him to meet us at the hospital," said Mum suddenly calm.

Mike ran out, "Come on Amy, hold on to me. Just breathe you're fine," she took me by the arm and led me out.

Once in the car, she fastened the seat belt around me as Mike jumped in the back.

"I just called Luke and Tara too," he said. "I thought you'd want me to."

"Thanks Mike," Mum started to drive. I felt every bump in the road and then these terrible pains started. Maybe I was plain stupid but I hadn't thought about contractions.

"Oh god oh god," I cried out. "We're almost there Amy," said Mum calmly.

"Ahh noo, I can't," I shouted.

"Here Amy, take my hand." Mike reached out his hand to mine in the front and I grabbed it and squeezed it with all my might. I couldn't help it.

When we arrived at the hospital, two nurses came out with a wheelchair and took me in. Mum and Mike walked along beside me, I screamed out in pain. I thought I was going to die when they put me on to the bed and took of my clothes and put me in a gown. I couldn't say any words, I couldn't even think. All I could do was feel and all I felt was pain. Everything was about to change.

Just a Day in Time

"I know I'll never settle," said Tara.

"Yeah you never will," nodded Lily reaching for some garlic bread. It was summer and we were spending the week with Lily's grandparents by the sea, we were out for dinner ourselves on our last night.

"I'm afraid I'll always be looking for more," I said.

"But what about Luke?" asked Lily, "do you not feel he's enough, even now?"

I was silent, he was enough but that wasn't what I meant.

"I think Amy means in life," offered Tara.

"Yeah, like I'm afraid I will always want more."

"That's not a bad thing, you'll achieve things that way," said Lily. "I'm afraid that I'll always be too afraid, too afraid to try even."

"No Lil," I said, "you have to try."

"I know and I do, but only the easy things you know? I never step outside of my comfort zone."

"It's scary," said Tara.

"What scares you the most?" I asked the two of them.

"Easy," said Lily, "not having you two."

"That terrifies me too," I agreed. "Tara?"

"Me too of course but also I guess I'm afraid of always being too scared to let people see the real me."

"What do you mean?" I asked.

"I mean I put up a wall, I fake things and I lie and I always tell myself I'll stop but I don't and I'm afraid I'll live my whole life in fear of what others would think if they knew the real me."

"People will love," said Lily, "don't we?"

Tara smiled and then said, "And you Amy?"

"I'm afraid of breaking my own heart," I said slowly, "with my decisions, I think I screw up a lot of my chances in the mindset that if I mess it up then I can't get hurt because it was my mistake. It's a twisted logic," I shrugged and sipped my water.

"Okay, I've a question," said Lily, "ten years' time, where are we?"

"Oh okay I love these," said Tara, "so we will be 27."

"I'll have met my man definitely," said Lily, "and we will be just about to move in together. Oh I'll be engaged. I always wanted to get engaged at twenty six."

"Hahah you're crazy, but I agree. I want my perfect man and I want us to live in a big city, not London but maybe New York or Sydney. We will have a little apartment together and I'll be acting in shows every-night and we will always have after parties to go to together," said Tara.

"But we will all live close," said Lily, "and even if we don't we have to have an annual holiday together and when we do have kids they will all know each other. At one stage we will all live together single in like a city and we can go out every night and have nights in with pizza and movies," said Lily.

"I think that'll be in our early twenties, like maybe during college," I said, "that would be the best, imagine the three of us in our own apartment."

"You in ten years then?" asked Lily.

In all honesty I didn't like to think about the future much. It scared me too much because I knew the future involved change and right now I had my two best friends, I had Luke and I had my family and I didn't want any of that to change.

"I've always wanted a penthouse," I offered.

"Hahah you're ridiculous, give us something solid. Come on, where will we find you, where can we send our letters to?" joked Tara.

"Just me," I said. "I don't know guys, all of that scares me, in all honestly in my future I just want to have great people and I just want to be as happy as I am, right here, right now."

"I'll raise my glass to that," said Lily, Tara raised hers too. "Spot on," she said.

"To the future," said Lily.

"To the future," we echoed.

Chapter 24

It felt like my mind woke up before my eyes dared to open. My hand flew automatically to my belly; deflated, flat. Well not fully but compared. My eyes fluttered open, taking in my surroundings. It was very bright but there was Luke, lying face down asleep at the bottom of my bed, his hand resting on my leg. Mum and Dad were at the bottom of the room, their backs to me talking in whispers to Deborah; who was holding a massive bouquet and basket. To my right Mike head was asleep on Tara's shoulder. His red-rimmed eyes looked down at my old teddy that was nestled in her lap, she was smiling. I didn't say anything, for a moment I just wanted to soak in this feeling of overwhelming love. I felt safe. I wanted to carry this feeling with me through whatever the future brought. I thought of the baby.

"Hello," I croaked out, my throat dry and parched.

"Amy!" exclaimed Mum waking Luke and Mike up. Suddenly, they were all around me: Mum stroking my hair, Tara babbling excitedly, Luke grabbed my hand.

"How are you feeling Amy?" Deborah's strong voice boomed over the noise. She smiled at me knowingly. I smiled back thankfully.

"Where's Alice?" I asked, sitting upright in my bed and looking around.

"Right here," said a voice coming into the room and suddenly amongst them all there was Dr Foster, holding my blue-eyed baby in her arms.

"I had to come in to see you, then I passed this one in the hall and I just couldn't resist having a peek. When we heard all the excitement down here we just rushed to join the party didn't we little one," she cooed over Alice, bringing her towards me. I reached out my hands and took her. She looked up at me so innocently; I had always thought babies were ugly until I saw her. I just loved her immediately. It felt like I already had.

After a little while of us all taking some pictures and turns holding her; I asked if Luke and I could just have a moment alone with Alice.

Everyone nodded; Tara kissed my forehead and then Alice's.

"I'm so proud of you," she whispered before following everyone else in silence. I moved over in the bed and Luke sat up next to me. A tear slid down his cheek as we held Alice together.

"She's ours Amy," he whispered, playing with Alice's closed hands. Her eyelashes were fluttering but she was staying so silent.

"Isn't she beautiful?" I said. We sat in silence. The warmth of his body radiated onto me and Alice.

"I'm so scared Luke," I finally said. He held me tight.

"We can do this," he spoke, "whatever this involves; I know we're strong enough. I love you enough."

I smiled nostalgically; for some unknown reason that was how I felt; nostalgic.

"She's a little mixture of you and me," I said, "isn't that crazy Luke. She's our love, mine and yours in a person."

I looked at him. "God, I love you," he said laughing.

"Always in all ways," I grinned back, cheesily.

"I know we spoke about it before Amy but I believe now more than anything we can do it. I promise to be here no matter what."

I nodded. I believed him, he would. Luke knew I needed a few minutes alone with Alice; he always knew these things so he got up to leave, kissing Alice's head.

When I was all alone in the room I spoke to Alice. I told her everything about her, me, Luke and everyone. I told her how she happened and how she was a surprise. It felt like rain after a long drought to speak all of those unspoken words. She looked up at me with her big blue eyes the whole time and didn't make a sound. I like to believe a part of her understood me, even though I know that's probably impossible. I said I was sorry countless times, I wasn't really sure what for but I told her how happy I was that she was here now. How I'd never felt such an attachment to a soul before. Her little fingers were wrapped around mine. Holding as tight as her little muscles could. I knew, for the first time in forever, exactly what I had to do.

The End.

Epilogue

It's been ten years since that cold February day. It's been ten years of joy, pain, choices, loss, happiness, but most of all it's been ten years of life. My world didn't collapse on that day, even though I was sure it would at any given moment. No, my life didn't end. Even though I believed I would be branded for the rest of my life, I thought I would always feel the loss; that my past would be etched onto the skin of my face and any stranger would glance at me and see a terrible, messy past, grimace and keep on walking. That day didn't ruin my life, since then I've learned nothing can. It just changed it. Who knows where I would be had it not happened to me, but see that's what we can never do, we can never really make fully informed decisions as we have no past life to learn from or no future life to perfect it in. We just do our best, and that's what I did. I did my very best. The day Alice was born I filed her for an adoption. My parents, as you know, only ever wanted what was best for me, and when I made the choice I knew it was the right one. She would be ten now. I got sent a photo of her for the first few years and I just know from her smile that she has a wonderful mum. I couldn't have been that for her, not then. No matter what people tried to tell me, I had nothing to offer her as a parent. I was still a child myself. Perhaps some people may see it as selfish but I wanted to live my life. After having Alice in August I took some time to myself, in a way I mourned the sense of everlasting youth I knew I would never taste fully again. But I was young and malleable and the greatest thing about life is we can never be irreparably broken so I pulled all my pieces together and started fresh. I got a job in a coffee shop. I still had my offers from London University but I didn't know anymore if nursing was right for me, I deferred for a year. Then one day I saw a sign on the notice board looking for volunteers to answer help lines on weekday nights. I went to the centre that evening and half an hour later I was sitting at a desk beside many others answering a phone. Something clicked with me, over the coming weeks I went to the centre every night. I really worked well just offering an ear to women suffering violence, kids scared their parents were going to split. I even got a call from a sixteen-year-old girl about to have an abortion. I did my research and I found a course in the University of Copenhagen, it was human rights specialising in women's rights. I applied and in July I got a letter in the mail confirming my entrance. I didn't know how to feel, I would be leaving behind London and all the places and people I loved, but at the same time I could start fresh. I had this chance, this chance to not forget about what happened to me and what I did, but this chance to move on from it. So I took it.

I know your all wondering what happened to all those people in my life, most importantly Luke and Tara. Luke and I stayed together, for a while, as you know we loved each other very much and we had a child together, nothing could ever break that bond. As I said when Alice was born, there was now a little mixture of Luke and I out there in the world, and to me there is no other way to show how much our love for each other meant; than to pass our love to another human being. It will live forever this way. We broke up about four months after Alice was born. Our paths were headed in different directions no matter what had happened. It broke my heart for years, his too. After a few years of contact we just couldn't bear it anymore and we decided to leave contact for a while. I still miss him but I know some people will stay with us forever and out of all the people in the world that my heart will never forget, I'm so very glad it's him.

Tara lived out her dream. She went to theatre school in London and in the last year or two she has made it big time. She's now touring as a lead in West End's Matilda. She's started going around to secondary schools teaching eating awareness workshops too with a group of women from the clinic she went to for recovery.

As for Crystal; I never heard from her; despite my continued attempt at contact. Then one day; when I had just moved to Copenhagen; Mum called me to say she had seen a death notice in the paper. A young girl named Crystal Walker had fallen from her 40th storey apartment in Hackney. It was unclear whether the incident was accidental or on purpose. No family was there to witness. This news hit me hard; because in ways I viewed, and still view today, Crystal as my alter person. The person I so easily could have been and the awful things that happened to her that I was just lucky to have not experienced. She taught me a lot and I will never forget her. I also thank her, because if it weren't for her; I probably would have had the abortion on March 15th and although I know that wouldn't have been a bad thing; I also know I'm so happy with how it all did work out and the lessons I learned.

Just because Lily and I fell out; doesn't mean she wasn't a fundamental person in my growing up. Sometimes I miss her, she's contacted me a few times and once we even went for coffee when I was back in London; but we're different people. Our lives have drifted too far for us to ever go back together, she was important to me though, she showed me and taught me a sort of kindness I've tried to carry with me. She got married last year and now she lives in Kent, working in elementary schools teaching music now as far as I know.

As for me, well now I live in San Francisco. I've been here for two years now. I've made friends, not many of them know about Alice, I don't hide it but I don't broadcast it either. I've met a guy, his name's Lucas and he's a painter, with his own gallery downtown. I haven't told him much about my life yet, healings a long process but as Dr Foster once told me; life is long and we have so many years to try and try again.

I write letters to Alice, one ever year. I don't know if she'll ever see them; I keep them in a box. The necklace Luke gave me is in there too, for her. Maybe one day we will meet and she can read all about it; maybe we won't.

Whatever happens, I've come to realise that Deborah was right in that hospital waiting room all those years ago. Our lives do lie in circumstance, and luck and chance but choice; well that's up to us. At the end of the day, I'm alive, Luke's alive and Alice is alive. We're not together in the traditional sense, but we will never be apart.

Some people will say I made a mistake, they'll say I will be haunted by this for the rest of my life, that I won't be able to forget and that not a day will go by that I won't think of her. They're right, not a day does go by that I don't think of Alice, but they're wrong, I'm not haunted by my past and yes I won't ever forget it but that's okay because it's my past, it's me and I don't want to forget, I want to be okay with remembering.

The End.